Socialistic Labor Party

Three Stars

Socialistic Labor Party

Three Stars

ISBN/EAN: 9783337409395

Printed in Europe, USA, Canada, Australia, Japan

Cover: Foto ©Andreas Hilbeck / pixelio.de

More available books at **www.hansebooks.com**

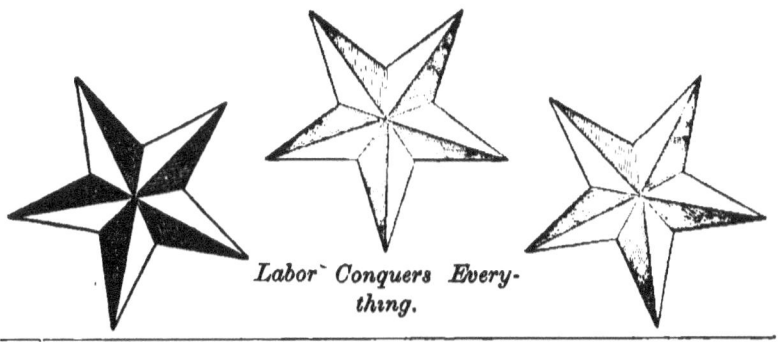

Labor Conquers Everything.

VOL. 1. No. 1.   DETROIT, MICH., JANUARY, 1880.   PRICE SEVEN CENTS.

COMPETITION.

COMPETITION for the people is a system of extermination. Is the poor man a member of society or an enemy to it? We ask for an answer.

All around him he finds the soil occupied. Can he cultivate the earth for himself? No; for the right of the first occupant has become the right of property.

Can he gather the fruits that the hand of God ripens on the path of man? No; for, like the soil, the fruits have been *appropriated.*

Can he hunt or fish? No; for that is a right which is dependent upon the Government.

Can he draw water from a spring inclosed in a field? No; for the proprietor of the field is, in virtue of his right to the field, proprietor of the fountain.

Can he, dying of hunger and thirst, stretch out his hands for charity to his fellow-creatures? No; for there are laws against begging.

Can he, exhausted by fatigue and without refuge, lie down to sleep upon the pavements of the streets? No; for there are laws against vagabondage.

Can he, flying from his native land, where everything is denied him, seek a means of living far from the place where his life was given him? No; for it is not permitted you to change your country except on certain conditions which the poor man cannot fulfill.

What then can the unhappy man do? He will say, "I have hands to work, I have intelligence, I have youth, I have strength—take all this, and in return, give me a morsel of bread."

This is what the workingmen do say. But even here the poor man may be answered: "I have no work to give you." What is he to do then?

What is competition from the point of view of the workingman? It is work put up at auction. A contractor wants a workman; three present themselves.

Boss—How much for your work?

First man—Two dollars; I have a wife and children.

Boss—Well; and how much for yours?

Second man—One dollar and a

quarter; I have no children, but I have a wife.

Boss—Very well; and now how much for you?

Third man—One dollar is enough for me; I am single.

Boss—Then you shall have the work.

It is done, the bargain is struck. The lowest bidder gets the job. And what are the other two workmen to do? It is to be hoped that they will die quietly of hunger.

But what if they take to thieving? Never fear, we have the police. To murder? We have got hangman.

As for the lucky one, his triumph is only temporary. Let a fourth workman make his appearance strong enough to fast every other day, and his price will run down still lower; then there will be a new outcast, a new recruit for the prison, perhaps.

Will it be said that these melancholy results are exaggerated?— that at all events they are only possible when there is not work enough for the hands that seek employment?

But we ask, in answer, does the principle of competition contain by chance within itself any method by which this murderous competition is to avoided? If one branch of industry is in want of hands, who can answer for it, that in the confusion created by universal competition, another is not overstocked? And if, out of 50,000,000 people, twenty are really reduced to theft for a living, this would suffice to condemn the principle.

But who is so blind as not to see that, under the system of unlimited competition, the continual fall of wages is no exceptional circumstance, but a necessary and general fact?

Has the population a limit that it cannot exceed? Is it possible for us to say to industry—industry given up to the accident of individual egoism and fertile in ruin—can we say, Thus far shalt thou go and no further?

The population increases constantly. Tell the poor mother to become sterile, and blaspheme the God who made her fruitful, for if you do not the lists will soon become too narrow for the combatants.

A machine is invented; command it to be broken, and anathematize science, for if you do not the thousand workmen whom the new machine deprives of work will knock at the door of the neighboring workshops and lower the wages of their companions. This systematic lowering of wages, ending in the driving out of a certain number of workmen, is the inevitable effect of unlimited competition. It is an industrial system by means of which the working classes are forced to exterminate one another.

If there is an undoubted fact, it is that the increase of population is much more rapid among the poor than the rich. Poverty, the fruit of competion, produces destitution. This is shown by statistics. Destitution is fearfully prolific. This is shown by statistics. The fruitfulness of the poor throws upon society unhappy creatures who have need of work and cannot find it. This is shown by statistics.

At this point society is reduced to

a choice between killing the poor or maintaining them gratuitously,—between atrocity and folly.

This point society has reached. Shall we build more poor houses, houses of correction, prisons, and penitentiaries? Shall we tax ourselves still heavier for the purpose of increasing our poor fund? How foolish, how suicidal, is any such course. Rather let us apply the antidote for the demoralizing effects of competition; and this is CO-OPERATION,—a co-operation that will embrace the whole nation. The means of production, public transportation and communication—land, machinery, railroads, telegraph lines, canals, etc.,—must be placed under popular control, thus abolishing our competitive and wages system and substituting in its stead CO-OPERATION! Let us all do our duty in hastening this glorious reform.

THE LAND QUESTION.

This proposition, that all mankind have an equal right to the surface of the earth, to the treasures which nature has deposited in it, and to the improvements which all the former generations have made upon it, is one not very difficult to prove correct inthe abstract. In fact, all the best thinkers of the English speaking peoples have admitted its correctness. Blackstone says: "We seem to fear that our titles (to the land) are not quite good; it is well the great mass obey the laws, without inquiring why they were so made and not otherwise."

We all know that what gives a man a legal claim to a given piece of ground, in the United States, is a chain of titles, which goes back to the time when these United States took possession. But since then many generations have passed away. But hear what our own Jefferson says of such a title: "This earth belongs to the living to use, not to the dead; our dead ancestors or grantors have no right now over the land, no power to say whom it shall belong to." Herbert Spencer claims, that the establishment of private ownership in the land was the greatest wrong that ever was done to mankind; was, in fact, a rascally act of robbery, and that the misery we see all around us will never cease so long as such private ownership obtains. And John Bright lately told the House of Commons of England, that "private ownership in land in this country (England), is the root of all our misery."

Land, on principle, is on the same footing with air and water. I have a right to that certain quantity of air which I inhale and use in my lungs; as soon as I exhale it, it becomes public property. So with land. It is therefore not wrong,—and in order to understand the land reformer's claim it is important to mark the difference,—it is *not* a wrong, we say, that a farmer who possesses 160 acres of land, or a man who has got house and a lot in the city, claim not to be disturbed; they have a *right* to occupy and use their respective parcels, as long as they need them. *But it is a wrong*, that a person who ten years ago bought a piece of land for a trifle, to-day may be a rich man, because the surrounding property has been improved, though he may have suffered his particular parcel to lie waste. This is, indeed, nothing but a shameful fleecing of the community.

It is a wrong, that a man who to-day buys a parcel of land, to-morrow may be a millionaire, because the rich mines or petroleum wells are found on the property,—treasures of which no human soul dreamed when the owner entered into possession.

It is a wrong—a grievous wrong—that a man who owns a block of houses in a populous city can pass a luxurious life thousands of miles away, without doing a day's work, simply because the law gives him the power of forcing from his numerous tenants the value of that property every ten years.

The same thinkers, however, who admit these wrongs, do not know any way of righting them. So Herbert Spencer says: "There are so many difficulties in the way' of making land common property, that I do not see any means of overcoming them. Had we to deal with the parties who originally robbed the human race of its heritage, we might make short work with them." Yet it is just as easy to abolish the present ownership in land, as it was to abolish slavery; we even contend, that it can be accomplish with less evil consequences. Suppose in a year

from now a majority of the people of this country should decree: "The fee to all real estate in these United States is hereby declared to be and remain in the said United States. All titles in fee in private persons are hereby abolished." What would be the consequence? Not a single person need be ousted from the premises which he occupied and used. The owners would simply be turned into tenants of the State, merely the name of payment to the commonwealth would be changed from "taxes" into "rents." Undoubtedly in other respects the change would be tremendous. Land, as private wealth, and a source of it, would disappear like mist before the morning sun. The occupant could no more sell it, no more mortgage it, no more derive incomes from it in the shape of rents. Land would lose its speculative, but retain its intrinsic value. Land held for speculative purposes would certainly be dropped. But occupants in good faith could use it as they do now; and when they could not use it any more and had to quit possession, they would be entitled to compensation for the improvements they might have made. It will thus be seen that the realization of the reform programme will not violate equitable interests.

"But how are you going to compensate the owners of the land for its present value, for the money which they have paid for it?" our opponents will here ask us.

We certainly admit that, if, as we fervently hope, this great change will be effected peaceably, the present owners will be indemnified for whatever improvements they have made ; or that, at least, if it is to be effected by force, those that support the reform will be compensated. But what then? Cannot the same nation that spent $6,000,000,000 to deliver a foreign race out of slavery, not raise, if necessary, $1,500,000,-000 to liberate the great majority of its citizens, especially when it will receive the consideration for the debt, the land itself, into its own hands? And it must not be forgotten that when the Industrial state is fully established as it must soon be after the land has become public property, all profit and all interest will cease; that consequently no money will further be paid in discharge of debts to domestic citizens, but only means of living and enjoyment.

"But," say our opponents again, "you will never entice the farmers into offering you their lands on such terms."

We reply: Wait only a little; wait until farmers have been reduced to the position of tenants, as in England and Ireland; and that will come before long. But we hope to have a majority of them within our ranks long before that.

POVERTY.

THE present arrangement of society, as respects an equitable distribution of property, is an utter failure. If this seems too sweeping an assertion, let it be tested. Let the objector look around him and note the enormous mass of evils which might be, and are not, prevented. Let him observe that the benefits, both moral and physical, realized under the present system, are wretchedly meagre, and that the means by which even this trivial good is gained are at the same time productive of grievous wrong.

The greatest evil resulting from the present social order is *po.verty*. Property is proclaimed to be the reward of labor and frugality. But is it so? Is wealth *prima facie* evidence of individual thrift? By no means. Statistics show that not one in a hundred of the most highly civilized people in Europe holds for his own use any property worth naming. The masses have nothing but their daily bread, and that always of inferior quality, often in insufficient quantity, and *no assurance that they are to continue to have it at all.* Says John Stuart Mill, "The condition of numbers in civilized Europe, and even in England and France, is more wretched than that of most tribes of savages who are known to us." And America under the same industrial system is rapidly being reduced to the same condition.

To say that no one should complain of this because it may be accounted for on natural grounds—

the weakest being trodden down in the general struggle for existence— is to offer no alleviation of the misery, even if the explanation were correct. If some Nero or Domitian were to require a hundred men to run a race with the announcement that the hindermost fifty or twenty should be put to death, it would be no extenuation of the despot's cruelty that the nimblest and the strongest would be certain to escape. What though ninety and nine fleet runners secure their lives, it were still an atrocious crime that one man should die because he could not run as swiftly as ninety-nine others. So, if there be any who suffer privation or degradation, any whose natural wants are not met, or met with such supplies only as might be adapted to satisfy a brute, this, though not necessarily the *crime* of society, is at least its failure. And to assert a a mitigation of the evil that those who suffer are the weak, is but to add insult to misfortune. Is weakness then an offense to be punished? Rather does it not appeal to society for protection against the suffering it cannot itself avert? If the prosperous were fair minded would they accept prosperity if for its possession even one innocent person must be excluded from a desirable existence?

There would be no ground of complaint on this score against society as now constituted, if every one willing to labor and abstain in reasonable measures could obtain a fair share of the good of life; but the fact is, that benefits and rewards, instead of being proportioned to toil and self-denial, are in most instances in inverse ratio to them. *Those who labor and abstain the most receive the least.* Even the idle, the reckless and the vicious poor—those who have only themselves to blame for their want—even they often work harder not only than the well-to-do but than most of those who by honest service earn the highest wages. Moreover, even the partial self-control exercised by the industrious poor costs them such an effort of self-denial as is seldom made by the better classes of society. "The very idea of distributive justice," says Mill, "or of any proportionality between success and merit, or between success and exertion, is, in the present state of society, *so manifestly chimerical* as to be relegated to the regions of romance."

The system under which society is now organized, *is hostile to its own interests;* for by it those who direct labor—a small minority—are enabled to monopolize, and *do* monopolize the means of production. The inevitable result is poverty and want for the many, power and wealth for the few. Socialists therefore declare that as poverty is so nearly universal and but remotely connected with desert, the present arrangement of society is a failure.

Socialists also affirm that there is but one remedy for this evil—a reconstruction of society. As poverty is the direct result of the present system, *this system must be abolished and a better one introduced.* How? BY THE UNITED POWER OF THE MASSES, THROUGH THE INSTRUMENTALITY OF THE BALLOT, SUPPLANTING COM-

PETITION BY CO-OPERATION. "The resources of life,—the means of production, public transportation and communication, — land, machinery, railroads, telegraph lines, canals, etc., must become, as fast as practicable, the property of the whole people, through the government abolishing our present competitive system and substituting in its stead co-operative production, and a just distribution of its rewards."

Labor being the source of wealth, and useful labor being possible only through association of effort, the means of labor should be in the hands of society, and not be held by a fraction of it. And since the leading political parties have always truckled to the monopolists, it becomes the duty of the working people to organize a great labor party which through political power shall achieve industrial independence.

This is the grand aim of Socialism: the abolishing of poverty by securing to every person through co-operation an opportunity to work, and all the proceeds of that work. Is not this object worthy of the countenance and support of every honest man and woman? Then let every voter join its ranks and by his ballot help hasten the dawn of that golden era—the Socialistic State,—the Industrial Republic.

HOW CAN LABOR IMPROVE ITS STATE.

Now, as it would be futile to expect on the part of the poorest and most ignorant of the population self-denial and prudence greater than that actually practiced by the classes above them, the circumstances of whose life are so much more favorable than their's for the cultivation of these virtues, the conclusion to which I am brought is this, that, unequal as is the distribution of wealth already in this country, the tendency of industrial progress—on the supposition that the present separation between industrial classes is maintained—is toward an inequality greater still. The rich will be growing richer, and the poor at least relatively poorer. It seems to me, apart altogether from the questions of the laborer's interest, that these are not conditions which furnish a solid basis for a progressive social state; but having regard to that interest, I think the considerations adduced show that the first and indispensible step toward any serious amendment of the laborer's lot is that he should be, in one way or other, lifted out of the groove in which he at present works, and placed in a position compatible with his becoming a sharer in equal proportion with others in the general advantages arising from industrial progress.— *Cairne's Political Economy.*

War is robbery; trade is swindle. —*Benjamin Franklin.*

Labor creates capital before capital employs labor.— *Wakefield.*

THE SOCIAL PROBLEM.

ALL the problems labor reformers propound may be reduced to two principal problems: 1. To produce wealth ; 2. To distribute it. The first problem contains the question of labor. The second contains the question of wages. In the first problem the question is of the employment of force. In the second of the distribution of enjoyment. From the good employment of force results public power. From the good distribution of enjoyment results individual happiness. By good distribution we must infer not *equal* distribution, but *equitable* distribution. The highest equality is equity.

From these two things combined —public power without, individual happiness within — results social prosperity. Social prosperity means men happy, the citizen free, the nation great. Society has solved the first of these two problems. She creates wealth wonderfully. But how about its distribution? We see all about us evidence of how badly this is done. John Stuart Mill spoke truly, when he wrote concerning the distribution of the products of the laborer: "Those who do nothing get the largest share; those who work the hardest, the smallest share." Thus this solution which is complete now only on one side—the side of production—has led inevitably to two extremes: *Monstrous opulence; monstrous misery.* All the enjoyment to a few, all the privation to the rest; that is to say, to the people;—privilege, exception, monopoly, feudality, springing from labor itself;—a false and dangerous situation which founds public power upon private misery, which plants the grandeur of the state in the suffering of the individual. A grandeur ill-constituted, in which all the material elements are combined, and into which no moral element enters.

The two problems,—the production of wealth and the distribution of it,—must be solved together to be well solved. The two solutions must be combined and form but one. And when that is done misery will be at an end; the unjust preying of the strong upon the weak will be no more; the products of labor will be adjusted mathematically and fraternally to labor; gratuitous and obligatory instruction, industrial and educational, provided for all; science will be the basis of manhood—the intelligence developed while the arm is occupied; and property democratized, *not by abolishing it, but by universalizing it,* so that every citizen, without exception, will be a proprietor. Then will have been ushered in the Industrial State—the Co-operative Commonwealth—the Industrial Republic; and material and moral grandeur will be combined.

"Labor existed for centuries before capital," is a saying of President Lincoln worthy of remembrance by all.

THE CONVICT.

———o———

BY VICTOR HUGO.

At the beginning of October, 1815, and about an hour before sunset, a man travelling on foot entered the little town of D— It would be difficult to meet a wayfarer of more wretched appearance; he was a man of middle height, muscular and robust, and in the full vigor of life. He might be forty-six to forty-eight years of age. A cap with a leather peak partly concealed his sunburnt face, down which the perspiration streamed. His shirt, of course yellow colico, fastened at the neck by a small silver anchor, allowed his hairy chest to be seen; he had on a neck-cloth twisted like a rope; trowsers of blue ticking, worn and threadbare, white at one knee and torn at the other; an old gray ragged blouse, patched at one elbow with a rag of green cloth; on his back a large, new, well-filled knapsack, and a large knotty stick in his hand. His stockingless feet were thrust into iron-shod shoes; his hair was cut close, and his beard large. Perspiration, heat, travelling on foot, and the dust, added something sordid to his wretched appearance. His hair was cut close, and yet was bristling, for it was beginning to grow a little, and did not seem to have been cut for some time.

On reaching the corner of the Rue Poichevert, he turned to the left, and then proceeded to the Mayor's office. He went in, and came out again a quarter of an hour after.

There was at that time at D—— a capital inn, with the sign of the Cross of Colbas. The man proceeded to this inn, which was the best in the town, and entered the kitchen, the door of which opened on the street. The landlord, on hearing the door open and a stranger enter, said without raising his eyes from the stewpan.

"What do you want, sir?"

"Supper and a bed," the man replied.

"Nothing easier," said mine host. At this moment he looked up, took in the stranger's appearance at a glance, and added, "For payment."

The man drew a heavy leathern purse from the pocket of his blouse, and replied:

"I have money."

"In that case I am at your service," said the host.

The man returned the purse to his pocket, took off his knapsack placed it on the ground near the door, kept his stick in his hand, and sat down on a low stool near the fire.

While the new comer had his back turned to warm himself, the worthy landlord took a pencil from his pocket, and he then tore off the corner of an old newspaper which lay on a small table near the window. On the white margin wrote a line or two, folded up the paper, and handed it to a lad who seemed to serve both as turnspit and page. The landlord whispered a word in the boy's ear and he ran off in the direction of the Mayor's house. The traveler had seen nothing of all this, and he asked whether supper would be ready soon. The boy came back with the paper in his hand, and the landlord eagerly unfolded it, like a man who is expecting an answer. He read it carfully, then shook his head and remained thoughful for a moment. At last he walked up to the traveler, who seemed plunged in anything but a pleasant;

"I cannot make room for you, sir." he said.

"What do you mean? Are you afraid I shall bilk you? Do you want me to pay you in advance? I have money, I tell you,"

"It is not that."

"What is it, then?"

"You have money?"

"Yes," said the man.

"But I have not a spare bedroom." The man continued quietly: "Put me in the stables."

"I cannot."

"Why?"

"The horses take up all the room."

"Well," the man continued, "a corner in the loft, a truss of straw; we will see to that after supper."

"I cannot give you any supper."

This declaration, made in a measure but firm tone, seemed to the stranger curious. He arose

"Nonsence, I am dying of hunger. I have been on my legs since sunrise, and have walked twelve leagues. I can pay and demand food."

"I have none," replied the landlord

The man burst into a laugh, and turned to the chimney and to the oven.

"Nothing. Why, what is all this?"

"All this is ordered."

"By whom?"

"By the carriers."

"How many are them?"

"Twelve."

"There is enough food here for twenty."

The man sat down again, and said "I am at an inn, I am hungry, and so shall remain."

The landlord then stooped down, and whispered with an accent which made him start "Be off with you."

The stranger at this moment was thrusting some logs into the fire with the ferule of his stick, but he turned quickly, and as he was opening his mouth to reply, the landlord continued in the same low voice; "Come, enough of this. Do you wish me to to tell you your name? it is Jean Valjean. Now, do you wish me tell you who you are? On seeing you come in I suspected something, so I sent to the police office, and this is the answer I received. Can you read."

While saying this, he handed the stranger the paper which had traveled from the inn to the office and back again. The man took a glance at it, and mine host continued after a moment's silence:

"I am accustomed to be polite with everybody, so pray be off."

The man stooped, picked up his knapsack, and went off. He walked along hap-hazard, keeping close to the houses like a sad and humiliated man. He did not look back once;

had he done so he would have seen the landlord of the Cross of Colbas in his doorway surrounded by all his guests and the passers-by, talking eagerly and pointing to him; and judging from the looks of suspicion and terror, he might have guessed that ere long his arrival would be the event of the whole town. He saw nothing of all this, for men who are oppressed do not look back, as they know only too well that an evil destiny is following them.

He walked on thus for a long time, turning down streets that he did not know, and forgetting his fatigue, as happens in sorrow. All at once he was assailed by hunger: night was approaching, and he looked round to see whether he could not discover a shelter. The best inn was closed against him, and he sought some very humble pot-house, some wretched den. At this moment a lamp was lit at the end of street, and a fir-branch hanging from an iron bar stood out on the white twilight sky. The traveler not daring to enter by the street door, slipped into the yard, stopped once again, and then timidly raised the latch and entered the room.

"Who's there?" the landlord asked.

"Some one who wants a supper and a bed."

"Very good. They are to be had here."

He went in, and all the topers turned to look at him. They examined him for some time while he was taking off his knapsack. Said the landlord to him, "Here is a fire; supper is boiling in the pot; come and warm yourself, comrade."

One of the men seated at the table was a fishmonger, who, before entering the pot-house, had gone to put up his horse in Labarre's stables. This fishmonger had been half an hour previously one of the party surrounding Jacquin Labarre, and had told his unpleasant encounter in the morning to the people at the Colbas. He made an imperceptible sign to the landlord from his seat, and the latter went up to him, and they exchanged a few whispered words. The man had fallen back into his reverie.

The landlord went up to the chimney, laid his hand sharply on the man's shoulder, and said to him:

"You must be off from here."

The stranger turned and replied gently, "Ah, you know?"

"Yes."

"I was turned out of the other inn."

"And so you will be out of this."

"Where would you have me go?"

"Somewhere else."

The man took his knapsack and stick and went away. As he stepped out, some boys who had followed him from the Cross of Colbas, and seemed to have been waiting for him, threw stones at him. He turned savagely, and threatened them with his stick, and the boys dispersed like a flock of birds. He paused in front of the prison, and pulled the iron bell handle; a wicket was opened.

"Mr. Gaoler," he said, as he humbly doffed his cap, "would you be kind enough to open the door and give me a night's lodging?"

A voice answered, "A prison is not an inn; get yourself arrested, and then I will open the door."

Night was coming on apace; the cold wind of the Alps was blowing. Worn out with fatigue, and hopeless, he sat down on a stone bench at the door of a church. An old lady who was leaving the church at the moment saw the man stretched out in the darkness.

What are you doing, my friend?" she said.

"You can see that I am going to sleep," he answered harshly and savagely.

"On the bench?" she continued.

"I have had for nineteen years a wooden mattress, and now I have a stone one," he replied.

"Why do you not go to the inn?"

"Because I have no money."

"Doubtless you are cold and hungry, and some one might take you in for charity."

"I have knocked at every door."

"Well?"

"And was turned away at all."

The good woman touched the the man's arm and, pointing to a small house next to the Bishop's palace, she continued, "Have you knocked there?"

"No."

"Then do it."

[To be Continued.]

A FABLE.

"A FATHER had a family of quarrelsome sons. When he failed to heal their disputes by exhortation, he gave them a practical illustration of the evils of disunion. He told them to bring him a bundle of sticks. He then placed the faggot in the hands of each of them in succession, and ordered them to break it. They each tried with all their strength, and were not able to do so, but took the sticks separately and broke them easily. He then said: 'My sons, if you are of one mind, and unite to assist each other, you will be as this faggot, uninjured by all the attempts of your enemies; but if you are divided among yourselves, you will be broken as easily as these sticks." This fable forcibly illustrates the trades unions of this city. They are the separated sticks and easily broken, but were they united to assist each other they would be uninjured by the attempts of their enemies. There is no need of so many labor organizations in this country. One is sufficient—and better. Let the object of every trades unionist be to bring every union under one head, so their combined action will be felt; but their actions must ever be founded upon abstract justice. Discuss this idea in your meetings and you will begin to learn the benefits that will accrue from such an organization.

WE wonder if those papers that cry out about our great prosperity would give their compositors, reporters and editors more wages if they asked for it? Gentlemen, take the hint and try it.

NOTES BY THE WAY.

Mr. Parnell wants the English government to buy out the landlords and sell the land in small parcels to the tenants, the government to bond itself to the landlord and the landlord to draw the interest. Why not leave him in possession of the land and draw rent? The robbery of rent is no worse than the robbery of interest. The farmer and wage worker of Ireland will have to pay interest then as well as they now have to pay rent. Mr. Parnell should not advocate such a measure, for why should the Irish farmer buy that which belongs to him? If a man steal a cow is not the owner doing society a wrong and putting a premium on crime if he crave the privilege of buying it back? To buy the land would recognize the right of the landlord to it, a right which does not exist. No man has a right to land who does not improve and till it. Otherwise it is not only morally wrong but economically disastrous, to which the present condition of Ireland testifies. John Stuart Mill says that "the reasons which form the justification in an economical point of view of property in land are only valid in so far as the proprietor of land is its improver. Whenever the proprietor ceases to be the improver political economy has nothing to say in defence of landed property. In no sound theory of private property was it ever contemplated that the proprietor of land should be merely a sinecurist quartered on it." The same author also says that "landed property in England is thus very far from completely fulfilling the conditions which render its existence ecomically justifiable. But if insufficiently realized even in England, in Ireland those conditions are not complied with at all." The Irish people should not parcel the land, but should enter into partnership and work it on a large scale. By that means they could afford the best of modern machinery and cultivate the land more effectively. The producing masses of the world should assist the Irish people to regain their inheritance. Let us in America do our share. We have no interest in common with England. Our interest lies in manknd.

Mr. Amos Fayram, of this city addressed several Unions in this city in regard to Workingmen's Savings Banks, and the result of one of these meetings was the appointment of a committee to investigate this system of Banks. The committee reported the week following in favor of the establishment of the bank worked on this system, and a provisional committee appointed to secure subscriptions to the capital stock. What has become of the committee? Waiting for the "workingmen" of Griswold street to subscribe capital?

The poverty of the masses is due to the fact that they eat too rich food, as meat and bread, and neglect the mush pot. If they would eat fried mush for breakfast, cold mush for lunch and boiled mush for supper, and put out at "interest" in "savings" banks all they receive over and above the cost of mush, they would all become rich—that is, if wages didn't drop to that point where there would be nothing over after buying mush.

WORKINGMAN, what is your idea of the labor question? Did you ever think of it beyond the mere matter of wages? Did it ever occur to you that wages could be abolished and that you could share in the legitimate increase of the wealth that your labor creates? It has been estimated that those who produce the wealth of the world receive only one-fifth of it. Where does the other four-fifths go?

THE shoemakers of this city have had a seeming increase in wages of five per cent. Some have an idea they are better paid than they were a year ago, when the fact is the contrary. The cost of living has increased about 25 per cent., wages five per cent., a reduction of actual wages of 20 per cent. And the newspapers tell us times are prosperous.

AT the Third Congress of the United States, held in Philadelphia in 1793, the Senate passed the following resolution: "Any person holding any office or any stock in any institution in the nature of a bank for issuing or discounting bills or notes payable to bearer or order, cannot be a member of the House while he holds such office or stock.' Carried out, ain't it.

PETER PAPIER, French philanthropist, has bought some 10,000 acres of land in Port Royal harbor, S. C., and proposes establishing a co-operative manufacturing city. He has already enlisted 2,000 persons in his enterprise. He possesses sufficient capital to meet the necessities of the colony that may arise.

IF some rich person should give every workingman in Detroit his flour, coal or wood *free* for five years, would not wages fall to just the amount saved by not having to buy flour, coal or wood? Reader, think this over, and see whether, *all other things being equal,* we are better off under high or lower prices.

O, WORKINGMEN! O, women! can you not see? Will you not hear? Can you afford to allow liberty to be lost? There is a deep plot to destry republican institutions in order to hold the masses in industrial slavery and perpetuate the power of the now threatened capitalistic supremacy.—*The Trades.*

THE average wages for labor does not exceed $1 per day. It therefore requires 1,180,000,000 days' work each year to pay industry's tribute to Shylock. Counting 250 working days to the year it requires the constant labor of 4,320,000 men to support in idleness and royal luxury a few thousand money sharks.

SOME workingmen in Chicago have organized on the co-operative basis, and this winter have saved over $2,000 on fuel alone. They then started a store with this saving. Why can't the workingmen of Detroit do likewise?

A large room in the third floor of Helsendegers Block, corner of Monroe Avenue and Farrar Street, has been secured, where all workingmen having a few hours of spare time either in day time or in the evening, can go and and amuse themselves in reading, games or conversation. It is proposed making this room a workingmen's headquarters. There is another large room on the same floor. Would it not be a good idea to have the trade unions of this city take hold of the matter, unite and use it as a room for their meetings? The expense will be much less than now, and all can have the full benefit of the club room.

LATELY Prof. Proctor predicted that in 250,000,000 years the earth would *grow cold* and expire. Immediately the coal dealers effected a combination and have already advanced the price $1 a ton. There's nothing like enterprise.

Co-operation in buying provisions will not solve the labor question. It will undoubtedly benefit those directly interested, because so few are now co-operators. The only solution to the labor question is National Co-operation.

MARCUS C. HEASLIP was elected the 3d inst. one of the delegates for Detroit Typographical Union in

ONE of the soundest labor papers in America is *The Trades*, published in Philadelphia, Pa., at 25 cents for three months or $1 a year.

WE commence in this number a story from the pen of Victor Hugo. The interest deepens with each succeeding chapter.

THE furniture workers of Chicago have started a co-operative factory; capital, $50,000, in 2,000 shares of $25 each.

WE want correspondents in every trade and labor organization. Items of interest to wage workers are solicited.

AN improved trade and increased cost of living justifies a demand for higher wages.

IN the last three months the cost of living has increased in this city 20 per cent.

WAGEMEN should all realize that overtime means under pay.

THE butchers' strike in Chicago has ended.

A FABLE. A wolf prowling around for a chance to steal a living, discovered a hen-pen and not being able to enter and devour the hens, made this compromise. "My dear hens, seeing I allow you to live on in this pen which I do not own, and I did not build, and as I am going

mulate their accustomed broods. So one night they appointed some of of their number to wait on the wolf and ask that they might have a few eggs left to them. The wolf refused and denounced them for their ingratitude. He told them that in consideration of fact that he had started the egg business, and that he had taught them how to lay eggs, and that he had kept them steady at work laying eggs; they owed him obedience as well as eggs.

He said the fox had advised him to eat the ring leaders. He had declined for the present, but would not promise for the future. At this the hens cackeled from fear; the noise awoke the farmer who owned the hens and the pen taking his gun, and shot the wolf and ever after the hens had peace.

Explanation.—The hens are the wage-workers; the wolf the devouring capitalist. The hen-pen is the world; the farmer is the awakend intellegence of the masses, who will some day arise and overthow the present swindling system of industry, through which a few reap the reward of which the many sow.--*Paterson Labor Standard.*

TERMS:

One year, in advance, - - 75 cents
Six months, in advance, - - 40 cents
Three months, in advance, - 20 cents
Single copies, - - - 7 cents

The name and address of subscribers should be written plainly, that mistakes may not occur.

Advertisements at the rate of 50 cents per square each insertion.

All letters should be addressed to

CO-OPERATING PRINTERS,
121 Porter street, Detroit, Mich.

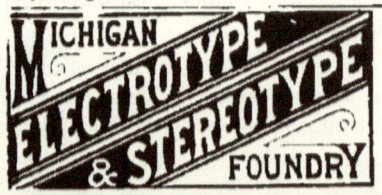

Labor Conquers Everything.

VOL. 1. NO. 2.   DETROIT, MICH., FEBRUARY, 1880.   PRICE SEVEN CENTS.

PROGRESSIVE STEPS TO INDUSTRIAL SELF-GOVERNMENT.

WHATEVER tends to place in the hands of the people the administration of their own affairs, is Socialistic in its very essence. When our revolutionary forefathers declared that all governments derive their just powers from the consent of the governed, they kindled a torch destined to burn forever, lighting up with its bright, pure rays the long-sought-for pathway to freedom.

It is now time to repeat that declaration in clearer and more explicit language.

All social institutions derive their existence and binding force from the consent of society. When society withdraws consent or recognition, any social institution must fall. The right to destroy an institution carries with it the right to establish new ones. It is the right of might!

The greatest of all social institutions is that of private property, and to show the point at which property ceases to be private, and becomes public in its nature, is to furnish the key to the solution of the Labor Question. The right of every indi-

own property is unquestioned, *provided*, that in so doing he does not interfere with the right and oppor-. tunities of others to enjoy equal advantages.

Property, the value of which depends upon the associative support of the public, and which without such support would be worthless; property, whose management affects public interests either for good or evil; property, which in private hands gives its possessors undue political and social power over the public at large,—all such property should be controlled by the public for their own protection.

This distinction must be clearly understood: Whatever is used to supply personal wants, whatever is needed for comfort and sustenance, such as houses, clothing, furniture, food, literature, works of art, etc., —all this is private property. But the use of any of these articles as commodities, *for purposes of profit*, is against public interest, not merely because all profit is robbery, but because the competion in buying and

sult in the impoverishment of the great majority of the people, and the destruction of all free institutions.

Political liberty cannot long continue where industrial monopoly corrupts public servants and dictates to the man of labor the ballot he shall vote.

The aim of Socialism is therefore to make the people, collectively and individually, masters of their own labor and opportunities through association. It is already a well known fact that wherever a large number of people combine their efforts and money in productive or distributive co-operation, they can successfully compete with and drive out individual capitalists. And when the municipality, county, State or nation, uses its vast forces of men, and immense resources, to conduct any great public enterprise, the capitalists are driven out of the field. Already the water-works, gas-works, and public schools of our large cities, and the postal and money order system of our national government, show how independent of private capitalists the people can be. The street railroads and coal distributive agencies of cities, and the railroads, canals, and telegraph lines of the nation, must next be taken in hand. Banking and insurance, now so abominably misused under capitalistic control, will soon be managed by the government. These are our present radical political demands. But the necessity of educating the debased, plundered and down-trodden working people is the most important preliminary step

Until the practical questions of life and labor are brought home to them in a manner easily understood, they remain easy tools of capitalistic politicians. When they comprehend the identity of interest between all classes of mechanics, whether skilled or unskilled, when they realize their power of association, as taught in the centralized and progressive trades unions, and in all movements for productive and distributive co-operation, then they will learn the value of the ballot and appreciate the necessity of industrial self-government. They would be inconsistent and blind indeed, if after the knowledge thus acquired they should vote to perpetuate politically the capitalistic institutions which in the shops and in every walk of life they are constantly rebelling against.

We must be patient and persevering, remembering that Society must *grow* into new conditions, and cannot jump into them; and that our greatest present task is to get society upon the right path. This once assured, the future is ours.

PHILIP VAN PATTEN.

THE United States have, since 1862, given to six railroad companies bonds to the amount of $65,000,000 besides a vast empire of land; and have also paid for the capitalists composing these companies $36,000,000 to these same or other capitalists as interest on these bonds.

A MAN who is intimate on short acquaintance, is almost sure to be "short" on intimate acquaintance

COMMON SENSE FOR WAGE WORKERS.

MAN and woman wage-worker, are you satisfied with your position in the world? Is your work certain, under all contingencies? Is your pay all that you desire? Does it give you the necessaries and refinements of life? No! not in one case in a thousand. You know that you ought to have better pay, and work less hours, to properly enjoy life. You know that you are little better than a slave, with the constant view of being turned adrift to starve. For when work and wages stop, everything stops, and despair gnaws constantly at your heart.

Perhaps your ancestors have been wage workers for generations, and your posterity may have the same fate. For it is the tendency of the existing social system, with its class divisions into employers and employed, to perpetuate a hereditary wage class, the most inferior class in the community, in respect to intellectual development, social position and the comforts of life.

There ought to be no such class in any society termed civilized. It is a relic of barbarism. It is only ancient slavery under another name. There is no longer any necessity for class divisions and class dependence, of the world, of all grades, are now able to carry on the business of the world, and practically do so. There is no longer need for outside classes, whose whole business seems to be to grasp all the profits, which by right belong to the workers.

The giant wrong of the age is class dependence. It gives up the masses to social slavery, takes from them the wealth which they create, dooms them to numberless disabilities, and is a perpetual bar to a true manhood and womanhood.

We have passed through five or six years of what are called "hard times." Tens of thousands of good men and women have suffered terribly—just as much as if we had been in the midst of war, and the Nation overrun by an enemy. Of what value is a social system where peace has no pre-eminence over war?

Getting down to the marrow of the thing, we had a public enemy, and that enemy was the money-power. No matter whether times are good or bad, this money-power is always gorging itself on the plunder of the masses. It has power to unsettle business and reduce values. It manipulates federal and state governments, and constantly adds

every bond and dollar that it has were blotted out of existence, the nation would be no poorer, for nothing would be lost but cunning instruments for popular plunder.

There is no longer any excuse for the inaction of wage-workers, and no longer cause to despair. Socialism offers them a remedy for all their wrongs, not through a plunder of the rich but the industrial independence of the poor. That is to say, that in the near future all production and distribution must be carried on by the toilers themselves, without the intervention or control of outside classes.

This industrial self-government, carried out through the general cooperation of all trades and industries, will necessarily give to the workers all that they create, and ultimately bring all classes into one. For it is an outrage on all rights to compel one class to support another in ease and affluence, while the worker himself goes half naked and has half rations.

Capital must compromise with labor, on some equitable basis, · that will relieve labor from dependence, add to its pay and reduce its hours of work. The times are full of danger to established abuses. A tyrannical and defiant capital will be met by a defiant labor. Labor, pointing to the vast accumulations of capital, can truthfully say that they were created by labor. Capital can only defend itself on the plea of custom and social usages. The accumulations are there, in possession of capital, and yet capital created

open to the enormity of its wrongs, how long will labor tolerate usages and customs which plunder it day by day, and constantly tend to consolidate a capitalistic tyranny which becomes more effective as it gains increase?

Labor is patient and long-suffering. It accepts the work-house as a pauper when it can toil no more, and the prison when its necessities have urged it to break the laws. It has no police or bayonets to intimidate refractory employers. But every wrong and strain can only reach a certain point, and the good of society demands that justice be done before that point be reached. Labor courts no anarchy or violence. Its terrible suffering through long strikes attest its peacefulness. Capital, "is they servant a dog," and will it continue to suffer as a dog?

Let every man and woman permeate themselves with the great truths of Socialism. They must read its tracts and hear its speakers. It offers them the wealth which they themselves create, abolishes class distinctions and mastership, and ushers in an era of peace and enjoyment. The plunder and abuses which labor suffers, must be put an end to. The people have the same right to reconstruct society as to change a form of government. Time sanctifies neither wrong nor robbery.   J. F. BRAY.

FORCE is the accoucheur of every old society which is pregnant with a new one.—*Karl Marx.*

PUBLIC prosperity has for its first foundation the culture of the earth.

THE PRINCIPLE OF UNITY.

"UNITED we stand; divided we fall," is a proverb in common use among others than co-operators, embodying the experience not of this age or country only, but of other times and men subjected to widely differing circumstances. The Bundle of Sticks, which has become its familiar illustration, is an old Greek fable; and has its analogue among the literature of other people who have given voice by their writings to the teachings of their lives. Every one instinctively feels its force in its application to the concerns of nations, the great world of politics. We know at what a cost of blood and of money Italy has attained of late years the unity for which her patriots have sighed for centuries. We may trace the same aspiration in Switzerland, where the opposition to it, fanned by theological differences, led over a quarter of a century since to a civil war, though, hapily for the Swiss, it ended with the first battle. Lancashire, Eng., has certainly not forgotten the cotton famine—that consequence of the struggles of the North to uphold the unity of the republic against the separatist tendencies of the South, developed through the controversies occasioned by the institution of slavery. And we have seen the influence over Germany gained by Bismarck from the success attending his bold policy of cementing by "blood and iron" that unity which, in 1848, Germany had in vain endeavored to obtain by revolutionary

In the political world, then, the principle of unity has asserted itself as the true guiding star of humanity. And the tendencies of political action appear to be to enlarge the sphere of action of this principle by a system which may conciliate it with the opposite principle of separate action.

Now what, in political matters, men have been for ages thus continually tending to do, more and more perfectly, the system of co-operation seeks to introduce into the sphere of their daily life; their ordinary business; their buyings and sellings; the modes of carrying on work and of exchanging its results. Everywhere it aims at establishing the principle of unity. In other words—in every instance it would have matters decided by reason and justice, which is only reason applied to practical life. This is what the principle of unity means, what it always tends to at last, though it may set off apparently in a quite opposite direction. The object of co-operation is to set up institutions, and by the means of them to extend among mankind the sphere of reasonable action—that great principle of unity. Let us see how it goes to work. Co-operators say: "The let-alone system so loudly praised as the true condition of material progress, has been tried and found wanting. True, to a certain extent it cheapens and multiplies the things needed for man's use, and so far benefits him; but it distributes these things un-

just claims of those among whom the distribution is made. It is always saying, in sense very different to the original meaning of the words, 'To him that hath shall be given, and he shall have more abundantly; while from him that hath not shall be taken away even that which he seemed to have.' It makes of men the perpetual creators of enjoyments which they do not share, and heaps them up in towns where they forego the life in the free air and sunshine without receiving any other life worthy of living, in compensation. It produces an atmosphere of fraud and distrust in which healthy morality dies, and where only its superstitious counterfeit can thrive. And even its one boast of increasing the number and diminishing the cost of the things serviceable to man it fulfils very badly; for it has a tendency to diminish the amount of labor or capital available for the purpose of production, by a multiplication of that which is applied to distribution, not because it is really needed in order to bring the things distributed in the most convenient manner within the reach of those who want them, but because there are a great many people who think they can get a living by setting up a shop more easily than in any other way."

The co-operators therefore have

amount of power for entering upon other more difficult reforms can be obtained. It is easiest to make, because it asks of those who engage in it only to do what is entirely in their own power—to concentrate their own consumption on some centre of supply set up by themselves; and also, because the management of such a business is of itself the easiest of all business, requiring the smallest amount of capital to set it up, because the capital is turned over so much more rapidly than is generally the case in productive establishments, and the least amount of special training, because the things dealt in can be obtained in a state fit for use, with no other trouble than unpacking them and arranging them in suitable places. And yet the profit on these trading businesses is actually much higher than the profit on many manufactures, where the producer is often very well satisfied if he can get five per cent. on every transaction, while the grocer or draper usually gets from 15 to 20 per cent. So that the consumers, by applying the principle of unity to their own supply—that is, by having only as many centers of supply as are really wanted, and bringing their custom together to the same points— can realize large profits after paying all expenses and interest on capital

est of all, instead of leaving the regulating of it to what might chance to turn up, when every one simply seeks to benefit himself. You see it depends for its pecuniary success on the principle of unity, and this principle is at the bottom of all the moral good which may flow out of it. Let workingmen everywhere unite to make common arrangements for their own supply in the most convenient and least wasteful manner, and instantly every one will begin to feel an interest in the way in which his neighbor is supplied, for *this is also his own interest*. So they will be insensibly drawn together. The common management in supplying themselves will lead to common meetings for recreation or instruction, tea parties, or lecture or reading rooms, or libraries ; and will lead, as the principle grows, and towns get linked to towns by the feeling of common interest, to many more, pleasant, instructive or useful institutions, which none of them might be able to set up advantageously alone, but which they can bring about by acting together.

The extension of the principle of unity from the retail to the wholesale business can be accomplished by concentrating the custom of many stores in many districts in one central institution, and each district should concentrate the retail custom

acter, not distributive, but productive; which might be brought, through the wholesale center, into communication with the distributive societies; the latter serving as instruments providing remunerative investments for the capital accumulated by the former, while they in turn served as instruments for securing to the productive societies a certain and correspondingly remunerative market for their productions.

Thus would the principle of unity extend its beneficial action over both the great complimentary departments of labor, production and distribution; and linking together consumers and producers by a common interest, begin to fulfil its proper office of carrying to the highest attainable degree the material, intellectual and moral progress of mankind.

TO BE REMEMBERED.

As soon as the capitalistic production seizes agriculture, the demand for farm labor decreases in the same ratio in which the augmentation of capital increases. The more the soil is tilled by machines, the fewer laborers will naturally be required; and here it is not like in factory industry, where the discharged labor-

THE CONVICT.

BY VICTOR HUGO.

THE house at which the woman advised the man to knock was the residence of the Bishop of the place—M. Myriel. His palace and the hospital was side by side; one a spacious and beautiful edifice, the other a low, narrow, one-story building.

Three days after the Bishop's advent, he changed the palace into a hospital, and took up his abode in what was formerly the latter. "For," said he, "there has evidently been a mistake here; twenty-six patients have been crowded into five small rooms, while three of us are expected to occupy a house large enough for sixty."

The Bishop's private life was full of the same thoughts as his public life, viz., to help in every way possible the poor, the oppressed, the down-trodden. He gave freely of his sustenance to all who applied, living no better than his poorest parishoner.

His household consisted of his sister, Mademoiselle Baptistine, and one domestic, Madame Maglorie.

As the Bishop was busy at a great work on "Duty: the Duty or All to Each and Each to All," there was a violent knock at the door.

"Come in!" said the Bishop.

The door opened. It opened quickly, quite wide, as if pushed by some one boldly and with energy.

A man entered. That man, we know already; it was the traveller we have seem wandering about in search of a lodging.

He came in, took one step, and paused, leaving the door open behind him. He had his knapsack on his back, his stick in his hand, and a rough, hard, tired and fierce look in his eyes, as seen by the firelight. He was hideous. It was an apparition of ill omen.

Madame Magloire had not even the strength to scream. She stood trembling, with her mouth wide open.

Mademoiselle Baptistine turned, saw the man enter, and started up half-alarmed.

The man, leaning with both hands on his club, glanced from one to another in turn, and without waiting for the Bishop to speak, said in a loud voice:

"See here! My name is Jean Valjean. I am a convict; I have been nineteen years in the galleys. Four days ago I was set free, and started for Pontarlier, which is my destination; during those four days I have walked from Toulon. To-day I have walked twelve leagues. When I reached this place this evening I went to an inn, and they sent me away on account of my yellow passport, which I had shown at the Mayor's office, as was necessary. I went to another inn; they said? 'Get out!' It was the same with one as with another; nobody would have me. I went to the prison, and the turnkey would not let me in. I crept into a dogs kennel, the dog bit me, and drove me away. I went into the fields to sleep; I thought it would rain, and as there was no good God to stop the drops I came back to town to get the shelter of some doorway. In the square I lay down upon a stone; a good woman showed me your house and said: 'Knock there.' I have knocked. What is this place? Are you an inn? I have money; I will pay. I am very tired, and hungry; can I stay?"

"Madame Magloire," said the Bishop, "put on another plate."

The man took three steps, and came near the lamp which stood on the table. "Stop," he exclaimed, as if he had not been understood, "not that, do you understand me? I am a galley-slave—a convict—I am just from the galleys." He drew from his pocket a large sheet of yellow paper, which he unfolded. "There is my passport, yellow, as you see. Will you read it? See, here is what it says: 'Jean Valjean, a liberated convict, has been nineteen years in the galleys: five for burglary and fourteen for having attempted four times to escape. This man is very dangerous.' There you have it. Is this an inn? Can you give me something to eat and a place to sleep? Have you a stable?"

"Madame Magloire," said the Bishop, "put some sheets on the presently, and your bed will be made ready while you sup."

"True? What! You will keep me? You won't drive me away? a convict! You are a fine man! You are an inn-keeper, aren't you?"

"I am a priest who lives here," said the Bishop.

"Monsieur, Cure," said the man, "you are good, you don't despise me; you take me into your house, you light your candles for me. And I haven't hid from you where I come from and how miserable I am."

The Bishop touched him gently and said: "You need not tell me who you are; this is not my house, it is the house of Christ. This is the home of no man, except him who needs an asylum. Whatever is here is yours. You have seen much suffering?"

"Oh," said Jean Valjean, "the red blouse, the ball and chain, the plank to sleep on, the heat, the cold, the lash, the double chain for nothing, the dungeon for a word. The dogs are happier! Nineteen years! and I am forty-six! And now a yellow passport. That is all."

Meantime Madame Magloire had served up supper. It consisted of soup made of water, oil, bread, and salt, a little pork, a scrap of mutton, a few figs, a green cheese, and a large loaf of rye bread. She had, without asking, added to the usual dinner of the Bishop a bottle of fine old Mauves wine.

The supper was served on solid sil

After supper, however, he said: "Monsieur Cure, all this is too good for me; but I must say that the wagoners, who wouldn't have me eat with them, live better than you."

After supper the Bishop said to Jean Valjean: "You must be in need of sleep; I will show you to your room," and he conducted him to the only spare bed in the little house.

The man was so completely exhausted that he did not even avail himself of the clean white sheets. He blew out the candle with his nostril, after the manner of convicts, and fell on the bed, dressed as he was, into a sound sleep.

As the cathedral clock struck two, Jean Valjean awoke.

(To be continued.)

"GOD AND MAN A UNITY."

"God and Man a Unity, and All Mankind a Unity," is the title of a neat 96-page 12-mo. pamphlet sold by by B. F. Trembley & Co., under Russell House, Detroit. The author, in offering a new religious idea and new social and industrial order, treats of the present Christian dispensation, its theological ideas and social practices; the New Dispensation, its religious ideas and social requirements; the necessity for a new dispensation; and closes with an appeal to all classes.

Under the latter heading the author says: "The mass of wage-workers, men and women, demand the right to work for themselves and to receive just payment for it. Is there anything wrong in that? They demand that what they earn by their own labor shall not be taken from them by other classes, through interest and profit. Is there anything wrong in that? The right to toil and to receive the earnings of that toil, lie at the foundation of social reconstruction."

A circular accompanying the book work. "God and Man a Unity," is claimed to be a New Revelation, adapted to humanity everywhere. It presents a living idea, applicable alike to the present and future generations. It abolishes inordinate toil, poverty and misery. It elevates all and depresses none.

"Man is the monarch of the world, and it is just what he wills it and makes it. As the Mosaic Dispensation gave place to the Christian Dispensation, so the latter in turn must be superseded by a more advanced religious idea, accompanied by social changes in correspondence with it. The New Dispensation comes among us a deliverer, because adapted to modern progress and necessities. It has come in accordance with universal law, to perfect what preceding generations have left undone. Let us give it welcome. It is sorely needed by all classes, and is a savior that cannot be crucified."

The book will well repay reading, and its price, 25 cents, places it within the reach of all. Copies can be procured from this office.

See page 16 for terms of subscrip-

SOCIALISTIC MARCH.

Our foe is now at bay,
    Along with us to meet him;
But march in close array,
    For only thus we beat him.
When few we come he sneers us " No!"
    If thousands we
    And earnest be,
Then, even if unarmed we go,
No " lord" shall dare say " No!"

We do not thirst for blood.
    No thought of plunder leads us;
But from this time, by God!
    We want no man to fleece us.
The rich may have what now is theirs,
    Keep up their fun
    Till 'tis all gone;
But what from now we make no shares
Shall evermore be theirs.

They say that we are free.
    Yes, free to steal or hunger!
The poor were never free!
    But poor we'll be no longer.
Now cunning folks have all so nice,
    Are bowed at,
    Get all the fat;
The toiler, he can feast—his eyes.
Then it will be otherwise.

The home our wives shut up,
    That they may fragments gather,
The child works in the shop
    Competing with his father.
Such things our hearts cut like a knife:
    But we here vow
    To change that now,
And willing be to stake this life
For children, home and wife.

But how accomplish this ?
    The single man can't do it.
The State must help in this,
    For only it can do it.
The workers, they make up the State;
    They thus have right,
    As well as might,
To open wide for peace the gate,
And banish strife and hate.

Our flag ! Thou type of love !
    Of love for all mankiud !
Like unto Noah's dove,
    Thou herald'st peace to mankind.
'Tis glorious under thee to march,
    To win the strife,
    To lose the life.
We go for thee to build the arch
Of triumph ! Forward, march!

THE LOGIC OF FIGURES.

ACCORDING to a tabulated statement given in the Cincinnati *Enquirer* in 1877 the total non-professional adults of the United States were 11,828,530 and the professional 677,343. The Congress of that year consisted of 189 bankers or bank stockholders, 94 lawyers, 14 merchants, 13 manufacturers, 7 doctors, 1 mechanic and *no* farmer. The Senate was made up of lawyers. These figures are now but very little altered.

paid, besides being unprotected? Who wonders that the products of the farm hardly pay for their production?

One-half of the voters of the Nation are farmers, and not one of their number in Congress to represent them!

Millions of dollars annually appropriated, but not one penny for the industrial classes. No dividends, no subsidies, no land grants and no Credit Mobilier ever come to labor.

interest that support it. Professional men and non-producers have filled every department of the Government, and the result is the condition which exists to-day.

They have had a fair test and shown their incompetency.

Law is presumed to be founded on justice and common sense.

If an aristocracy is to rule, it matters not whether the Democrats or Republicans are successful.

Labor must organize to overthrow aristocracy. The entire labor element should combine into one harmonious body and ask professional aristocracy to step down and out. First unite; then educate; then act!

Labor has the brains, the numbers, and the muscle. To permit itself to be led, governed, enslaved, and robbed is disgraceful and cowardly.

Before justice can be done and liberty secured, workingmen must rule America!

NOTES BY THE WAY.

It is almost universally admitted that "fat" matter set in which all compositors in an office have not an equal opportunity of being benefitted thereby is an injustice and repugnant to the basic principles of unionism. The mutual benefit received is the cement which binds men together, and its adhesiveness increases in proportion as the benefits of *all* are enhanced. The benefit exists in bringing all as near as possible upon a common level, and destroying those inequalities which create dissatisfaction and inharmonious action; and those who do anything which tends to create this inequality are guilty of conduct injurious to all, and are consequently unfair. The equal distribution of "fat" has become a law by custom and by legislation from the International Union down to the humblest subordinate. Its justice is so evident that it hardly needs discussing, and should be patent to every candid mind. It

tends to equalize wages. It tends to increase wages. It equalizes opportunities, which is the object of all good and wholesome organizations, and which alone is the key to success. The principle deserves the support and strenuous agitation of every honest printer.

R. F. Trevelick addressed an eight-hour meeting in Kittleberger's Hall, Tuesday evening, Feb. 10th. Philip Van Patten, was elected chairman, and opened the meeting with a few well-chosen remarks, and was followed by Mr. Trevellick in a speech of over an hour, reciting the work done by the committee now in Washington; and giving good hope that with a little concerted effort on the part of the workingmen, together with the fact that we are on the eve of a presidential election, that Congress may be made to enforce the eight-hour law now incorporated in the United States statutes, for the benefit of workingmen, as faithfully as they have enforced the law for the contraction of the currency for the benefit of bankers and bondholders. Resolutions were adopted pledging the moral and financial support of the audience to the committee now pressing the matter on the attention of Congress, and emphatically declaring that they would kill politically any Congressman who voted against enforcing the law. Thos. Dolan, secretary of the meeting, was authorized to receive subscriptions and forward them to the committee at Washington.

ON Friday evening, Feb. 6th, a large number of carpenters met in the Workingmen's Club Room, cor. Monroe avenue and Farrar street, to take steps toward the organization of a Carpenters', Joiners' and Cabinet Makers' Union. Speeches were made by Messrs. Simpson and Labadie, recounting past experiences and and showing how future success can be achieved. The mention of a contemplated effort by prominent labor men to amalgamate all the trades in the city through a Trades Assembly, was vigorously applauded. Twenty-three persons signed the roll. The meeting then adjourned to meet Feb. 12th.

WE note with pleasure the move ment just begun by men prominent in the labor cause, toward the establishment in this city of a Trades Assembly. Detroit workingmen are sadly in need of such an institution. The inter-dependence of one trade on another, in this age of machinery, can be demonstrated in no better of the men of these trades and an interchange of ideas, desires and wants. For over five years the trade unions of this city have led a half-dead existence. Let us all lend a helping hand and with a strong pull, and a long pull, and a pull all together, do what we can to put more life, and strength, and hope, in our drooping organizations.

"BOOMING" is the only word that rightly expresses the condition of the Workingmen's Club Room, corner of Monroe avenue and Farrar street. A nice meal is given for ten cents; a cup of coffee or tea for three cents; and all the labor papers are thrown in free. Laboring men wishing to stay down town to attend meetings can drop in there and spend an hour very agreeably and profitably in discussing labor questions and exchanging ideas. Come, brothers, and give this practical enterprise your countenance and support by doing all in your power to make it a success.

IN competition capital buys labor. In co-operation labor buys capital. The whole distinction of principle lies here. Capital is used in co-operation and honestly paid for, but the capitalist is excluded. Capital is a commodity, not a person. The worker is the sole person concerned in co-operation. The capitalist sells his commodity to the co-operator. The capitalist has no position but that of a lender, no claim save for the interests for which he bargains, and, being paid that, he should not be permitted to reappear as a participant in the profits of labor. The

terest, has no claim to any more, any more than a landlord to a second rent, or a coal merchant to a double discharge of his bill.—*From Holyoke's History of Co-operation.*

THE newspapers, ministers and "charitable" people of this city are eagerly discussing the "new form of charity," as though people wanted that which should be abhored by all honest and intelligent people—this so-called charity. We don't want charity, we want justice. Teach the people that if they have the means but to support two children, that it is criminal and immoral to have more; teach the people that interest, profit and rent may be abolished by co-operation, thereby improving their material condition; teach the people that they must free their minds from the thraldom of superstition, and with the knowledge of these subjects will come justice, and with justice as the supreme factor in society the old and "new forms of charity"—or, in other words, alms giving—would fade away as the gray of dawn with the morning sun.

AT a meeting recently held in the Workingmen's Club Room, Hilsendegen Block, Monroe avenue, a gentleman took occasion to denounce Socialists for not supporting the

have been expected to support Greenback candidates when Greenbackers themselves did not. However, we are all working for the same end, and should employ our time more advantageously than by quarreling among ourselves. Let's hear no more of it.

ON the 2d inst. 15 drivers employed by the American District Carriage & Express Co. rebelled against the brutal regulations of the company. Their hours were from 7 a. m. to 12 p. m., for which they received $1 25. In addition to this they were compelled to buy liveries which cost $52. They did not complain of anything but the long hours, and acted in a sensible manner in striking for shorter hours. Workingmen should remember that shorter hours means more pay.

IT is equally obvious, however, that colonization on a large scale can be undertaken, as an affair of business, only by the government, or by some combination of individuals in complete understanding with the government.—*Mill.*

SOME narrow-minded bigots of this city refused to allow Hon. Robt. G. Ingersoll's portrait to be hung in their shop windows, as are those of other public personages. It is consoling to know that such actions but

There is one thing that all must take into consideration, namely, that the laboring classes are not by any means all illiterate and brutal, that they cannot be dictated to by preacder, politician, or editor, who assume an autocratic manner toward them, but that they are as a class, to be controlled by justice, and by a reasonable showing that they are fairly dealt with. We are not alarmists but who can say that Russian Nihilism, German Socialism, French Communism, with our unsettled political conditions, are not largely outgrowths of the injustice which power and money have done, and are now doing to the poor?—*Watch-Tower.*

Says an esteemed correspondent : "Who would have thought that blinded and despised Ireland would come to the rescue of the labor reform movement, and spread its idea throughout the world."

THE Fort Wayne, Ind., daily *Sentinel,* in view of the "prosperous condition " o f t h e country, has reduced the price of composition to 20 cents. A good printer, by close work, can make nearly a dollar a day.

WE look upon it as the height of absurdity to go on paying retail prices, which means three or four profits, when by combination on the co-operative plan we can buy at cost of production.

THE late Congress of the Socialistic Labor Party honored Detroit by choosing it as the headquarters of the Executive Committee of the

"THE problem of checking population is miserably evaded by all those who have meddled with the subject. If the superstitions of the nursery were disregarded, and the principle of utility kept steadily in view, a solution might not be very difficult to be found."—*James Mill.*

THAT only which is essential to the sustenance of life has inherent value, and the value should be regulated in the degree which it contains that essential element.

WHEN you hear anyone say that Socialists or Communists "want to divide," you may make up your mind that he is a fool—at least . as regards the aims of either.

A CORRESPONDENT writes: " Can you get me any work to do? I am willing to work for anything that will pay board. I am now working in a butcher shop for a dollar a week."

Laborers on the Detroit, Marquette & Mackinac Railway struck for an increase of 25 cents a day, on the 2d inst. They were getting $1 25.

Preparations are under way for a grand Beecher (Bread and Water) Banquet to come off soon at the Workingmen's Club Room. Don't miss it.

WE want correspondents in every labor organization. Items of interest to wage workers solicited.

A GOOD agent in each shop in the city, to canvass for subscriptions for this journal, wanted.

Work quiet in the printing busi-

Our complaint is not that brains rule, or that culture should lead, but that conscienceless, cunning, and miserly acquisitiveness are rewarded better than constructive ability or open-hearted integrity.

We complain that our rulers, statesmen, and orators, have not attempted to engraft republican principles into our industal system, and have forgotten or denied its underlying principles. We complain that statesmenship is narrow and partisan, the pulpit blind and ignorant, and the press the advertising channel of wealth. And while we thus suffer, fortunes are accummulated, wealth and power are centralized.

And while our masters are reveling in luxury, excelling the nobility of Europe in extravagant display, aping their manners and imitating their follies, we are becoming crowded down to the level of the "pauper" labor. of monarchical countries.— *Paterson Labor Standard.*

1. The *Fundamental Right* of the Citizen is INHERITANCE, natural and social.

2. The *Highest Duty* of the Citizen is LOYALTY TO THE COMMONWEALTH.

3. The *Central Idea* of Labor is ANTI-PROFIT.

4. The *Ultimate Destiny* of Labor

for that purpose, and not over 8,000,-000 are enclosed. Over 20,000,000 acres are held by land rings or individual monopolists for speculative purposes, in tracts of 125,000 td 300,-000 acres. This state of things has long been felt to be a great check to the prosperity of the State. Under normal conditions men of small means might be expected to flock in large numbers to settle upon the rich farming land, and healthy, active, and enterprising agricultural communities would arise; but this has been rendered impossible by the refusal of large land owners to sell except at exorbiant prices. The new Constitution seeks to remedy this evil by providing that the taxation of lands held in large uncultivated tracts shall not be assesed, as heretofore, at the nominal value of 50 eennts to $2,50 per acre, but that the same valuation shall be placed upon them as upon the small cultivated farms adjoying them. This will be from $20 to $60 per acre, according to location, and will make the annual tax on one of these small kingdoms $100,000 or more. Such assesments will soon cause the monopolists to sell their tracts for what they will fairly bring.

TERMS:

One year, in advance,	75 cents
Six months, in advance,	40 cents
Three months, in advance	20 cents

THE LABOR REVIEW.

Vol. 1. No. 3.   DETROIT, MICH., MARCH, 1880.   PRICE SEVEN CENTS.

THE LABOR REVIEW.

TERMS OF SUBSCRIPTION.

One year, in advance, - - 75 cents
Six months, in advance, - - 40 cents
Three months, in advance, - 20 cents
Single copies, - - - - 7 cents
The name and address of subscribers should be written plainly, that mistakes may not occur.

Advertisements at the rate of 50 cents per square each insertion.

All letters should be addressed to

CO-OPERATING PRINTERS,
121 Porter street, Detroit, Mich.

SALUTATORY.

WITH this number we present our readers a monthly in new style and name, being a combination in a neat and compact form of the nameless Monthly Magazine for workingmen and women and the *Bulletin of the Social Labor Movement.*

Our object, as indicated by the heading, will be to give a monthly review of the labor movement throughout the world, and the publication of short, vigorous articles on abstract economic justice. We will tell the truth and take the consequences, wage unrelentless war upon wrong, and champion the labor cause from a standpoint of right. The proceedings of the National Executive Committee of the Socialistic Labor Party will be published in these columns.

We are in hopes that our business will soon warrant us in enlarging THE LABOR REVIEW to twice its zine devoted exclusively to the interest of the industrial people of all climes and nationalities, and whose character will be first-class in every respect. tearing the mask from off our present false economy and displaying it in such a light as to make even those now blind see the folly of hugging to their bosoms this thing so hideous and so cruel. It will be to the interest of our readers to aid in lengthing our subscription lists and disseminating the principles advocated by THE REVIEW. We hope our friends will continue their patronage.

SLAVERY.

The White Slave and the Black Slave.

W. G. H. S.

THE wrong of slavery was the principle, sanctioned by law and defended by the church and by public opinion in the South, that, certain white men and women had a right to hold certain black men and women—and of course their children—as their *property*, and to use them as their *capital.* This was the wrong Garrison and Phillips denounced, and that the public opinion of the world (except where slavery existed) was finally brought to denounce. This change of public opinion ultimately brought about the great war that overthrew that tremendous wrong forever. The wrong was so vast in its dimensions, and there were so many powerful

indirectly interested in its mainte-
nance, that there was no other way
but that of war that could practically deal with it.

The labor question is just such a
question as the slavery question was.
Our present system of labor and business rests upon another great fundamental wrong with which there is no
way of practically dealing but by
the entire overthrow of the wrong
itself. The so-called abolition of
slaverly simply abolished property in
man; nothing more. The slaves were
no longer anybody's property. Their
status then became just the same as
that of all other non-propertied laborers the world over, just the same as
that of our own working men and
women.

What was the reason that slaves
were valuable property? What was
the object of the slaveholder in possesing slaves? They were owned
wholly and solely because they were
useful as capital. A man possessed
of them could make them work for
him. If he owned but one, he could
live an idle life himself. If he owned many, he could enrich himself
with the prducts of their labor. But
he could not take to himself all the
products of their labor. Slaves had
to be fed, clothed and housed, or they
could not have worked; they would
have been no use to him as capital;
in fact, they would have died.

So much for slave labor. The very
essence of it was that the slave had
to work for somebody besides himself; another man got all the products
of his labor except what was barely

his brawny limbs, able to work, but
with no house to shelter him and his,
only the scanty clothing on his back,
and even that not his, no food, no
tools, no cattle, no seeds, no lands!
In short, there he stood, as thousands
and millions of white laborers stand,
with ability and skill to labor, but
without possessing any of the means
of labor—without capital. Clearly
he must starve. He is so much capital without an owner.

"But," you say, "does he not own
himself? does he not own his ability
to labor?" Yes, perhaps; but ablity to
work and willingness to work are
not enough; he is without the means
of work. He has no land to work upon, or has no shop to work in, no tools,
no seeds or raw material; and nothing to live upon, and no place to live
in, until he has produced something
that he can exchange for these things
without which he must die.

"But," you say again, "if he cannot employ his labor himself, why
cannot he sell it? There is always
a certain demand for labor; he can
sell his labor at the market price."

Very true; so he can. He can hire
himself to another man, as it is called; that is, as you say, " he can sell
his labor." But our newly-emanci-
pated slave has had enough of work-
sng for other men; he wants to work
for himself and noboby else. He
wants all the products of his labor
for himself.

"Well, "you say," if he is so grasp-
ing as to want his own, and so fasti-
dious as to be unwilling to be another man's servant, let him hire some

rent; will nothing besides wear and tear be charged for these things, or for the tools? Will he get his seed, cattle and tools at cost without profit? In short, will not the man who does all this for him charge him for it in some way, and thereby obtain a part of the products of his labor—in fact, use him as capital? •

So do you not see that notwithstanding the abolition of slavery, the essence of slavery still remains.

"The man without capital has got to work for somebody besides himself."

This was what kept the slaves in ignorance and poverty, and the slaveholders in luxury and idleness, under the system of chattel slavery; and this same wrong is the true and allsufficient explanation of paupers, tramps, monopolies, and millionaires under our industrial system.

Under slavery, the fundamental error of principle was—the legal righ of property in man, the object being to use him as capital.

Under the present industral system, the fundamental error of principle is:—the legal right of property in man's inheritance; the resources of nature; and the accumulated results of man's progress in the past; indispensable for his progress in the present, and a sacred trust for future generations.

Happily, property in man has passed away. Not without a struggle. Next must follow, property in man's inheritance. The method of its abolition is the problem of to-day. It is

Will you be on the side of the Supreme Powers, or try to oppose them?

Are you in favor of a "strong goverment," a goverment of brute force in the interest of a few; or are you in favor of a "stronger goverment," a goverment of reason and justice in the interest of humanity?

AN EQUAL CHANCE.

Its Impossibility Under Existing Social Conditions.

JUDSON GRENELL.

To THE great majority of mankind life is a continual struggle for existence. All are striving, in what we call civilized countries, to lay by during the prime of manhood sufficient to provide for "rainy days" and old age.

Reader, look around you. What do you see? You see that of those engaged in this struggle for this noble end only a small number succeed. Now, is it true that though few succeed, yet those who fail have had "An Equal Chance?" We answer: IT IS NOT TRUE! Under our present competitive system, with its planless production and unjust distribution, there never has been and never can be "an equal chance." There can be no equal chances where there are unequal opportunities. The phrase is a most deceptive one, cunningly set afloat by those who profit by it in making the swindled portion of mankind think none but themselves to blame for their poverty and suf-

gard to what is commonly held as success in life, *i. e.*, leisure, abundance, education, influence. *The great majority are continued in the condition in which they are born.* Some are born to riches without work. Others are born to a position in which they can become rich by work. But the great majority are born to hard work and poverty from the cradle to the grave; and some are born to indigence.

The rich man's sons are born rich. The well-connected man's sons are born to opportunities to profit by the social position of their parents, and so grow rich by work. The poor man's sons inherit naught but their father's poverty. His wages being governed, not by the results of his toil, but by the average cost of sustaining a family of four in the way required by the standard of living in his class, the father is *compelled* to set his children to work earning their own living at just the time they should be at school, and when it would be the most beneficial to them. They are thus deprived of the benefits of an education, and so follow the tread-mill existence of their father. Generally a pauper is a pauper's child. A fatality follows the parent's misfortune or misconduct; and the father or mother a pauper, the child is also a pauper.

Next to birth the chief causes of success in life is *accident* and *opportunity.* When a person not born to riches succeeds in acquiring them,

phancy; by hard-hearted and close-fisted selfishness ; by the permitted lies and tricks of trade; by gambling speculations; often by downright knavery ? Energy and talents are of much more avail in life than virtues; and where one man succeeds by employing energy and talents in something useful and honorable, ten men thrive by using the same talents in some unjust way: in ruining a rival, or in fleecing those with whom they have dealing ; and in many ways, under the name of "business tact," bettering their pecuniary condition at others' expense. Says Mill: "Honesty, as a means of success, does not tell as much as the difference of a single step."

But suppose all had really "an equal chance," could all, under our present social conditions and class divisions, become rich ? *Most certainly not !* It takes the labor of at least ten men to make one man rich. That is, ten men must remain poor —must needs be deprived of a portion of their products, in order that one man may have an abundance. So, for one man to get rich, it is conditioned that nine remain poor. The exceptions to this are so few as to prove its correctness as a rule. If all should insist on getting rich by making others work for them, the result would be that there would be no one to work for another, and consequently no one would become rich. Notwithstanding this mathematical truth, the industrial sharpers and shylocks try to befuddle working-

scheme, ramifying all production and distribution, and embracing every race, creed, color and condition. Toward this the whole civilization of our race has been training us. One's success now mainly depends on the misfortune, loss or death of others. Now, as these inequalities and unequal chances are the direct and natural result of our present unjust social system, this system must be abolished *by the united power of the masses!* And here, in the United States, this power is already in the hands of the masses: the ballot.

As has been well said: "The resources of life,—the means of production, public transportation and communication, land, machinery, railroads, telegraph lines, canals, etc., must be placed, as fast as practicable, under popular control, through the government,* to gradually abolish the wages system and substitute in its stead co-operative production, with an equitable distribution of its rewards."

The people make their own laws collectively, why not make their bread collectively? They elect men to make their laws; why not elect men to take the superintendance of their industries,—their mines, mills, railroads? Why leave these important means of life in the hands of irresponsible parties whose only aim is personal aggrandizement, and who thus necessarily create and maintain inequalities that produce unequal chances?

Let us all stand shoulder to shoulder, and, marching in close ar ray, each do his duty in the battle now waging of moral right against pecuniary might. Then indeed will quickly dawn the day that will give all an equal chance by abolishing unequal opportunities.

---

* For the Socialistic idea of "Government," see Tract No. 2, issued by the So-

NIHILISM.

NIHILISM sounds in the ears of the vulgar and ignorant as the word Christian used to centuries ago, and Republicanism in France and Abolitionism in this country within our own memory. We are now thankful these came, for with them came more freedom, more justice. We meet with hundreds of fools in this country who grow pale when they hear of Nihilistic uprisings and "outrages," and who have not the fairness to investigate the reasons why these these things exist in Russia, nor the intelligence to know that tyrants or ignoramuses might as well try to dam the ocean as to try to stop the progress of thought and civilization. Most of the demands made by the Nihilists are enjoyed by ourselves here to-day, and for which the bloody battles of our own Revolution were fought. The contents of a captured Nihilistic newspaper are described in a telegram as follows:

The most important part of the contents is the programme of the Executive Committee, which is prefaced by remarks to the effect that the Russians are oppressed and taken advantage of by the present Goverment, and that the only way to gain reforms is to overthrow the Goverment by force, revolution or conspiracy. The Socialists will then transfer the reins of power immediately to an Assembly of Organization elected by all Russians without distinction of class or property. The Assembly of Organization will act according to the instructions of its constituencies. This is the general policy of the Socialistic Revolutionists, by which they throw in their lot with all oppressed Russians; but when the Assembly of Organization is elected, the Socialist party will recommend in that Assembly the following programme as its own:

1. Permanent popular representation, with full power over all general State questions.

2. Wide local self-government, with election assured for all duties, the independence of the rural commune and the economical independence of the people.

mune as an economical administrative whole.

4. The principle that the land is the property of the people.

5. A system of measures having in view the transfer of all works and factories to workingmen.

6. Complete liberty of conscience, speech, the press, public meetings, association, and electoral agitation.

7. General electoral rights without any conditional or property limits whatever.

8. Replacement of the standing army by a territorial army.

THE CONVICT.

VICTOR HUGO.

[For the benefit of new subscribers we give a short synopsis of the first two chapters of "The Convict," as follows: About an hour before sunset on an October afterternoon a man enters the town of D——. His aspect is forbidding. The inns refuse him admittance. He wanders around and at last is directed to the house of the bishop of the place, who gives him food and shelter. Jean Valjean is the man's name—a convict just free from a 19-year's sentence in the galleys.]

CHAPTER III.

JEAN VALJEAN belonged to a poor peasant family of La Brie. In his childhood he had not been taught to read, and when he was of man's age he was a wood-lopper at Faverolles. He had lost father and mother when still very young. All that was left Jean Valjean was a sister older than himself, a widow, with seven chidren. This sister brought Jean Valjean up, and so long as her husband was alive, she supported her brother. When the husband died, Jean Val-

wretchedness gradually enveloped and choked.

One winter was hard, and Jean had no work to do, and the children had no bread.

One Sunday evening Isabeau, the baker, was just going to bed when he heard a violent blow dealt to the grating in front of his shop. He arrived in time to see an arm passed through a hole, made by a fist, in the grating and window-pane. The arm seized a loaf and carried it off; The baker rushed out, pursued the thief, and caught him. It was Jean Valjean.

Jean Valjean was brought before the court of the day, charged with "burglary committed with violence at night in an inhabited house." He was found guilty, and sentenced to five years in the galleys.

He started for Toulon, and arrived there after a journey of twenty-seven days in a cart, with a chain around his neck. At Toulon he was dressed in a red jacket, and was no longer called Jean Valjean, but No. 24,601.

What became of his sister and the seven children? What becomes of the spray of leaves when the young tree is cut at the foot? It is always the same story. These poor living beings, these crhatures of God, henceforth without support, guide or shelter, went off hap-hazzard, and gradually buried themselves in that cold fog in which solitary destinies are swallowed up, that mournful gloom in which so many unfortu-nates disappear during the sullen

nal added three years to his sentence for his crime, which made it eight years. In the sixth year, he tried, but could not succeed. He was missing at roll call, the gun was fired, and at night the watchman found him hidden under the keel of a ship that was building, and he resisted the *garde chiourme* who seized him; this was punished by an addition of five years. Thirteen years. In his tenth year his turn came again, and he took advantage of it, but succeeded no better: three years for this new attempt, or sixteen years in all. Finally, during his thirteenth year he made his last attempt, and only succeeded so far as to be recaptured in four hours: three years for these four hours, and a total of nineteen years. In October, 1815, he was liberated; he had gone in, in 1796, for breaking a window and stealing a loaf.

Let us make room for a short parenthesis. This is the second time that, during his essays on penal questions and condemnation by law, the author of this book has come across a loaf as the staring point of the disaster of a destiny. English statistics prove that in London four robberies out of five have hunger as their cause. Jean Valjean entered the bagne sobbing and shuddering: he left it stoically. He entered it in despair: he came out of it gloomy. What had taken place in his soul ?

* * * * * * *

What aroused him? Was it that the bed was to comfortable ? Close onto twenty years he had not slept in a

silver forks and spoons and the great ladle which Madame Magloire put on the table. This plate overwhelmed him—it was there—a few yards from him. When he crossed the adjoining room to reach the one in which he now was, the old servant was putting it in a small cupboard—at the bed head. The plate was heavy and old, the big soup-ladle was worth at least 200 francs, or double what he had earned in nineteen years, though it was true he would have earned more had not the officials robbed him. He rose, and listened; all was silent in the house, and he went on tip-toe to the window, through which he peered. The night was not very dark; there was a full moon across which the heavy clouds were chased by the winds. This produced alternations of light and shade. After taking this glance, he walked boldly to the alcove, placed his knapsack on his shoulders, put on his cap, the peak of which he pulled over his eyes, groped for his stick, which he had placed in the window nook, and holding his breath and deadening his footsteps he walked towards the door of the adjoining room, the Bishop's.

The door yielded to the pressure, and made an almost imperceptible and silent movement, which slightly widened the opening. He waited for a moment, and then pushed the door again more boldly. It continued to yield silently, and the opening was soon large enough for him to pass through. Jean Valjean advanced cautiously and carefully, and avoided coming into collision with

basket, leaped into the garden, and bounded over the wall like a tiger, and fled,

* * * * * * *

The next morning at sunrise the Bishop was walking about the garden, when Madame Magloire came running towards him in a state of great alarm.

"Monseigneur, monseigneur:" she screamed, "does your Grandeur know where the plate basket is?"

"Yes," said the bishop.

"The Lord be praised," she continued; "I did not know what had become of it."

The bishop had just picked up the basket in the flower bed, and he now handed it to Madame Magloire. "Here it is," he said.

"Well!', she said, "there is nothing in it; where the plate?"

"Ah!" the bishop replied, "it is the plate that troubles your mind. Well, I do not know where that is."

"Good Lord! it is stolen, and that man who came last night is the robber."

The bishop remained silent for a moment, then raised his eyes, and said gently to Madame Magloire:

"By the way, was that plate ours? I had wrongfully held back this silver, which belonged to the poor. Who was this person? evidently a poor man."

A few minutes later he was breakfasting at the same table at which Jean Valjean sat on the previous evening.

As the brother and sister were leaving the table there was a knock at the door.

"Come in," said the Bishhp.

The door opened and a strange and violent group appeared on the the threshold.

Three gendarmes were holding Jean Valjean by the collar.

"Ah, there you are," said the Bishop, looking at Jean Valjean. "I am

the candlesticks too, which are also silver, and will fetch you 200 francs. Why did you not take them away with the rest of the plate?"

Jean Valjean opened his eyes and looked at the Bishop with an expression which no human language could render.

"My lord," the corporal said, "what this man told us was true, then? We met him, and as we thought he was running away, we arrested him. This plate——"

"Is his; I gave it to him," interrupted the Bishop. "You can let him go."

The gendarmes loosed their hold of Jean Valjean, and retired. The Bishop then walked up to him and said in a low, impressive voice, "My brother, never forget to employ this money in becoming an honest man. You no longer belong to evil, but to good. I have bought your soul of you. I withdraw it from black thoughts and the spirit of perdition, and give it to God."

Jean Valjean, stunned by the unexpected, softened by an act of kindness, the first for twenty years, fled from the presence of the Bishop. From that moment he was a changed man.

(*To be continued.*)

One of the greatest disadvantages we labor under at present is that under our present industrial system, working as we do, ten, twelve, or fourteen, or even more hours a day, we have so little time left for recreationor improvement, or the acquisition of that knowledge necessary to fit us for self-government. For this reason, if for no other, all should strive to establish a shorter legal work-day.

The produce of labor constitutes the natural recompense or wages of

THE HISTORY OF A CRIME

An announcement as above in the *News* brought together a good sized audience at the Workingmen's Club Room, corner of Monroe avenue and Farrar street, on Saturday evening, March 6th, to utter a protest in the name of the workingmen of Detroit, against the crime of imprisoning Messrs. Menton and McDonnell, of Paterson, N. J., the one for writing and the other for publishing a correct account of the treatment the laborers in a brick yard were subjected to by their employers. Appropriate remarks were made by comrades Goldring, Erb and Van Patten, and resolutions were passed expressing sympathy for Menton and McDonnell, and calling on all workingmen to take such steps as would ever put it out of the power of the capitalistic class to thus maliciously and wickedly punish labor advocates for complaining of the wrongs they endure.

LEGALIZED BRIGANDRY.

Men are deserving of credit when they create or produce from nature's resources, through their skill and industry additions to the sum total of national wealth. But when by the tricks of trade, or by means of special privileges acquired through favorite legislation, one man is enabled to strip ten thousand men of the fruits of their labor, it is little less than legalized robbery. The New York *Commercial Advertiser*

Hardly a dollar of this vast sum was produced or created by the men who accumulated it, and every penny was taken from wealth producers without a farthing's consideration. It required the labor of 400,-000 men daily, for a year, to earn this amount over and above the means of their subsistence. Without any increase in the aggregate wealth of the country, these ten men and firms were able to rake into their coffers eighty million dollars that were produced by,and justly belonged to, other men.—*Ex.*

THE BEECHER BANQUET.

On the evening of March 19 the Workingmen's club room was crowded with attendants to the bread and water banquet, which was given under the auspices of the club. Mr. E. W. Simpson was chosen chairman for the evening, and on taking the chair made a neat little speech on the subjects of bread and water and Beecher, which was followed with music by Prof. Undeutsch and a song, "The Old Sexton," by Mr. Kreighoff, of the Socialistic Mannerchor. The toasts and speeches came next, in the following order: "Discontent the Mother of Progress," responded to by Joseph A. Labadie; "The Minister as he is and the Minister as he should be," response by Judson Grenell; "Our Representatives in Congress," response by Henry A. Robinson; recitation of the "Song of the Shirt," by Miss Florence Bar-

Evil," response by Henry A. Robinson. The entertainment closed by the selling of the silverware (tin plates and cups), Henry Poole acting as auctioneer. The guests voted the entertainment the grandest success ever had in Detroit, and an occasion which will long be remembered. The newspapers pronounced it "a magnificent success." The proceeds went to the club room fund.

DETROIT TRADES ASSEMBLY.

MONDAY evening, March 15th, delegates from the carpenters, cigarmakers, shoemakers, painters, ship carpenters and caulkers, and printers met at Kittleberger's Hall, and proceded to the organization of a Trades Assembly.

E. W. Simpson, carpenter, was chosen temporary chairman, and Philip Van Patten, draughtsman, Secretary. A preamble and constitution was adopted, subject to the approval of the unions represented, and Mr. F. B. Egan, printer, was elected President until a permanent organization should be effected. The delegates then adjourned to meet Thursday evening at 65 Michigan avenue.

The above is a simple account of a meeting of great importance to the wage-workers of Detroit. It indicates an awakening on the part of our Unions to the necessity of closer relations with each other; to the fact that the ill or good fortune of one trade affects all other trades; and to the knowledge that where employers are tacitly united to keep down wages, employes must combine to keep them up.

Labor is the only universal, as well as the only accurate measure of value, or the only standard by which we can compare the values of different commodities at all times

THE MONTH'S REVIEW.

To GIVE an accurate list of all the strikes, lockouts and advances in wages that have taken place the past month would occupy too many pages of THE REVIEW. We can only give a short resume of the most important ones.

In Detroit but two strikes have occurred, one among the molders in the car works, and the other at the works of the other at the works of the Detroit Leather Company. Both were unsuccessful, owing mainly to insufficient organization on the part of the strikers. Thorough organization is a necessary preliminary to a successful strike. And with a well-conducted trades assembly to counsel and help individual trades a general advance of from 10 to 25 per cent. in wages in this city during the next six months will be an assured fact.

There are now 35 unions organized in St. Louis, Mo., acting together in their Trades Assembly and advanced wages and shorter hours are being brought about. The 15th of April is set down for a general strike in those trades not already receiving higher wages.

In Denver, Col., 21 unions are in existence, and the work still going on. A general strike occurred there a short while ago; and as the capitalistic papers have not reported a failure, it is safe to assume that it was entirely successful.

In California the Chinese question is the one uppermost in the minds of the people. "Chinatown," San Francisco, has been condemned by the proper authorities as a nuisance. The workingmen are determined that the clause in the constitution prohibiting the employment of Chinamen by corporations chartered by the State shall be enforced. U. S. troops have been ordered to San Francisco ostensibly to preserve the peace, but really to incite disturb-

attempt on the part of workingmen to enforce the law.

All through the Eastern States strikes are of daily occurrence, and almost uniformly successful. The one of greatest magnitude was at Cohoes, N. Y., of several thousand. They demanded ten to fifteen per cent. advance and 60 minutes for dinner. The proprietors said they would shut up their mills first; but finally gave the advance and 50 minutes.

The journeymen printers of New York city have demanded a general increase in wages, and are preparing to back it up. The pianomakers, also, are demanding an increase of wages, and are now on strike.

The impossibility of placing any reliance whatever on papers in the interest of the employing classes is so patent that it seems unnecessary to warn our readers against their opinions or reports of strikes, lockouts, etc.

The Nihilists of Russia, the Socialists of Germany and the Communists of France are all working for the interests of the producer as against the non-producer. Whether they work politically, or in some other way, it is sufficient if they help to equalize the figures as between what the wage-workers produce and what they receive. Even Ireland is lending its aid in opening the eyes of the people to the robbery perpetrated on them under our present land tenure system. May all these things "work together for good" to the advancement of the right and the final overthrow of oppression everywhere.

On our last page will be found the platform of the Socialistic Labor Party, which the Socialistic Tract Association will furnish at 20 cents a hundred or $1.75 a thousand, postage or expressage prepaid. Address orders to Judson Grenell, Sec'y,

NOTES BY THE WAY.

A cigarmakers' union has recently been form at Battle Creek, Mich.

COMPETITION is the life of trade. Co-operation is the life of industry.

Of all cant, the cant of the American pretending to disapprove of the Nihilists in Russia or the Irish in Ireland is the most disgusting.— *Wendell Phillips.*

REV. MR. LOCKWOOD, of Paterson, N. J., a couple of weeks ago read an essay before the New York Baptist ministers' meeting on "Christ's method of reaching the masses." It was a thoroughly communistic document, sound and sensible, and provoked considerable discussion.

A London paper, in tracing the mode in which 122 titled families in England have acquired land, states that scarcely a dozen of the number got them by professional or commercial pursuits. The writer asserts that not one-tenth of the 5,500,000 acres possessed by the 122 was acquired for value received.

SOME time ago a short communication in the *News* of this city brought forth a long editorial attempting to show that in the battle for bread all "had an equal chance." The article in this number of THE REVIEW, under the title "An Equal Chance," will, we hope, give labor advocates a few points in their favor on the question discussed.

WITH improved machinery and wise management and wise statesmanship, five hours' labor per day is sufficient to sustain life and surround it with comforts. If not, why and for what all this vast wilderness of machinery? What does its oceans of smoke mean? What does its interminable roar teach? Does it mean long hours, low wages, poverty, rags, destitution and social slavery? Under the rule of King Capital it has

At a general meeting of miners last week, it was resolved to work only eight hours a day after January 1, 1881.

THE fires of freedom are blazing brightly. The tottering monarchies of the old world are haunted by prophetic visions of an uprising of down trodden humanity that will bury them forever under the ruins of their crumbling thrones.

The New York piano manufacturers are beginning to weaken, and several firms request their men to return to work. You see the boom has caught the manufacturers with a light stock, and the men are determined to have their share of the "good times coming."

How much easier, and more pleasant it is to work together, to co-operate, than to work competitively, each one's interest continually clashing with that of the other. Take for example a watch, or any other piece of mechanism, if all the parts did not co-operate or work together, how long would they work at all?

REV. DR. EDDY visited the Workingmen's Club room, recently, and partook of dinner. If ministers mingled more with workingmen, they might be able to dispel the idea in the minds of most people that ministers are a lot of schemers, who neither believe nor practice what they preach. But this is expecting too much.

OUR civilazation is a farce; a delusion; a sham; a disgrace; a cunningly devised tyranny. Our goverments are the velveted throngs of capitalistic rule to drive the people into obedience and submission. Our laws are the barbarous edicts and utterances of the bought servants and hired dupes of the money-getting gangs who control our happiness. Do the wealth producers employ the wealth they create? Does the weaver her handiwork? Does the delver in the earth, the toiling handcraftsman in shop, mill and factory enjoy the wealth he produces.—*The Trades*

What are the common wages of labor, depends everywhere upon the contract usually made between those two parties (the employers and employes) whose interests are by no means the same. The workmen desire to get as much, the masters to give as little as possible. The former are disposed to combine to raise, the latter to lower the wages of labor. It is not, however, difficult to foresee which of the two parties must, upon all ordinary occasions, have the advantage in the dispute, and force the other into a compliance with their terms. The masters, being fewer in number, can combine much more easily.—*Adam Smith.*

STRIKES are the order of the day; and we notice that those are most successful where backed up by a strong labor organization.

Subscribe for THE REVIEW.

THINK IT OVER.

EDITOR LABOR REVIEW:

One thing we workers must make up our minds to do, if we really wish to emancipate ourselves from the present system of wages slavery, for what else can that be called which subjects us to the control of any one man, and that is that we must free ourselves from the habit of intemperance, which so curses this country. The best use for a nickel or a dime is not to invest it in beer or whiskey, which only brutalizes instead of refining and elevating us, but to support any movement which seems to afford a possibility of freeing us from our present dependent condition, and of raising us to a state of independence, of manhood, of true democracy.

SOCIALISTIC LABOR PARTY.

Summary of Proceedings of the Nat. Ex. Committee.

FURNISHED BY THE SECRETARY, PHILIP VAN PATTEN.

Upon suspension of the National Executive Committee at Cincinnati, by the Board of Supervision, a Provisional National Executive Committee was elected by the Section of Detroit, the city chosen for that purpose by the recent National Convention. The resolutions of that Convention were immediately laid before the Party for ratification, as was also the action of the Board whereby the Cincinnati membership was suspended, the election to be closed on March 10th.

During the period from Jan. 21st until March 10th, the Sections have been so engaged in discussing internal affairs that little has been done in the way of agitation. Correspondence with the sections give the following information:

The Section in Boston has had considerable disturbance, resulting in the withdrawal of the English-speaking members. They express dissatisfaction with the actions of their representative at the recent National Convention, who was recently elected Organizer of the Main Section. Not knowing the facts in the case, we avoid expressing any opinion, but trust that personal considerations will be dropped, for the sake of unity and harmony. The Section of Rockville has been revived, and promises active work. The movement in Lawrence, Mass., New Haven, Conn., and Providence, R. I., is reported sound, but traveling speakers are needed. The Brooklyn Section publishes a declaration to the effect that there is full harmony between their own and the New York Sections, and they will "*Union*" as soon as the party vote shall be found in favor of the plan. Caleb Pink refused to accept any nomination as our candidate for the Presidency, and publishes a card showing that he greatly misunderstood the nature of our movement, and that he disapproves the policy of organizing the working people for timely measures; but is in a hurry to establish Socialistic arrangements. The Baltimore Section has had some valuable agitation with the assistance of Comrade Osborn Ward, of Brooklyn. They have reorganized under the new Constitution, and better work is expected than was heretofore possible. The Wheeling Section has temporarily dissolved, owing to the opposition of a strong rival organization called the Labor Reform Party. Our men will, however, watch the ambitious leaders of that organization, and be ready at the first indication of a sell-out to set things once more to rights. At West Hoboken, N. J., the Section has been reorganized. Comrade Kuhl, of Paterson, N. J., recently an able agitator in Germany, is now active among his countrymen on this side the ocean, and promises to push organization throughout the entire State of New Jersey. Comrade Rossberg, of Courtney, Pa., states that a speaker is much needed in his district, where the workmen are nearly all miners, and belong to a secret society styled the Knights of Labor.

The Philadelphia Section reports their daily paper in good condition, and they are taking steps to organize the State of Pennsylvania, in which work the Sections of Alleghany City and Pittsburgh promise their active assistance. At Buffalo, N. Y., a new German paper has been started by Comrade Emil C. Erhart, with the title, *Die Lanterne*. He promises a new Section in that city.

consequence of their imprudent actions since they were temporarily suspended, the Board of Supervision has expelled the Section from the Party. This of course allows the minority, who disapproved the improper acts, to form a new Section, which it is hoped they will lose no time in doing. In the latter part of February Comrade Ehmann visited Lawrenceburg, Ind., a little town close to Cincinnati (once made holy by the presence of Rev. H. W. Beecher), and spoke before a good meeting of iron molders, called together by Comrade Michael McCarthy, who now resides in that place. In Louisville, Ky., there is a sad negligence on the part of the once active members. The failure of our daily paper there had the same effect upon the movement as was the case in Cincinnati: Personal quarrels, faction strife, mutual recriminations, etc. New men must take charge, and all mention of old difficulties must be rigidly suppressed. Time will no doubt heal up old wounds, and capitalistic oppression will unite the suffering toilers once more to fight the common enemy.

Indianapolis still contains a Section small but vigorous. The members have had the good sense to disregard the advice of our discontented friend Haller, and are helping the Trades Unions. There is still some bad blood on account of the refusal of our recent Convention to admit their delegate, C. A. Light. The Party vote has, however, sustained the action of the Convention, and we trust that even friend Lizius will, in time, admit that Party interests and Socialistic honor should be regarded as more worthy of consideration than technical formalities.

Detroit is always sound. Since the organization of the first Section in this city there has been the great-

Through the aid of our leading Socialists, a Trades Assembly has been formed, which promises to unite the entire working class of Detroit. A new Section of our Party has also been organized at Springwells, Mich., a suburb of Detroit. The Section will celebrate the anniversary of the 18th of March, 1871, by a mass meeting to be held Sunday, March 21st, at Arbeiter Hall. On April 10th a concert and ball will also be given at the same hall with the assistance of the Socialistic Maennerchor, whose recent entertainment received the highest encomiums from the leading newspapers and musical societies of Detroit.

In Milwaukee our daily paper has been enlarged, and now promises to be a success. It has considerable heated discussion with the paper edited by Dr. Sigel, once a warm (pretended) friend of Socialism but who now sells his talents and principles to the Republican Party. The Chicago membership are busily engaged in the Spring campaign, and hope to elect several new Aldermen and Town officers. The election occurs in April, and good results will be expected. The division among the Trades Unions has not yet been bridged over, though the leaders who forced the strife are now cooling off again. The new Trades Assembly, organized by Comrade Morgan and others, has drawn to itself the support of nearly all the unions, and is now firmly established, so that it is only a question of time as to how soon harmony will be restored.

The lesson of this contest is that so often demonstrated before, that jealous attacks upon men of honor who do their whole duty can only strengthen instead of weakening them.

St. Louis is the liveliest place in the country for the Trade Union

now powerful, and so enthusiastic that the town is hardly large enough to hold them. About forty Unions are in working order, all branches of industry being attended to, and a general strike is being talked of, the time being fixed for the month of April. Comrade McGuire has his hands full, and reports that there are from five to eight meetings every night, of one sort or the other, besides about fifteen different meetings on Sunday. Comrade Geo. Winter is active in the meetings, speaking every night.

Comrade Curlin, of the *Volks Stimme des Westent*, is about commencing a tour through the adjacent States, for purposes of organizing and gaining subscribers for the paper.

In New Orleans the Trades Unions and labor organizations have united through the Trades Assembly, and are now making the labor movement jump along. Comrades Carpenter and Geissler inform us that the Board of Trade and other capitalistic institutions have adopted resolutions welcoming the Chinese, who are being driven from California, and that the Trades Unions adopted counter-resolutions declaring that the pestilent heathens shall not pollute the State of Louisiana. The newspapers threaten the working men with all kinds of horrible fates if they attempt to "Kearneyize" the Chinamen, but the men are determined, and the hot-blooded southerners will evidently make it warm for "John."

The Section of San Francisco reports immense meetings, great excitement,. and rapid progress in the work of disseminating Socialistic principles. A collision with the capitalistic forces is daily expected, for the bosses are now the "rebels," and they refuse to obey the new Constitution, which prohibits the employment, by corporations, of Chi-

namen. Mayor Kalloch, who was elected by the workingmen, has made a silly exhibition of his ignorance and toadyism. He has endeavored to make peace with the monopolists, by declaring that he has no sympathy "with any form of Socialism or Communism." He also flatters the new "Citizen's Association" (the rebellious money grabbers and stock gamblers), and professes to consider their objects "laudable and well-meant." The Section has adopted resolutions denouncing the hypocrite, and will make his position decidedly warm for him. The action of Kearney, who is reported to have followed the Mayor's example, is most incomprehensible. Explanations are in order, and they cannot be delayed.

Result of the Party Vote.

The following is the result of the Party vote on the actions of the National Convention submitted to the Sections for approval or rejection:

ADOPTED.

The refusal to admit C. A. Light, delegate from the Indianapolis Section, to a seat in the Convention.

The adoption of the committee report approving the rebuke given by the Chicago Section to the National Executive Committee for having in June, 1878, advised party members to withdraw from all military organizations which claim to be Socialistic in principle, and which thereby compromise our party in the eyes of the public.

The adoption of the committee report approving the action of the National Executive Committee in declaring that our party has not and will not have any official connection with military organizations.

The sanction given to the proposition to establish a daily and weekly paper in the English language, in New York city, under the control of the New York and Brooklyn sections, and for which they will be responsible.

The name of the paper to be "Union."

Sections throughout the country to immediately make preparations for the holding of festivals, fairs, balls, etc., in aid of the proposed English paper.

Party papers which may publish attacks upon any party member before his case shall have been acted upon by the Board of Supervision, or the section to which he belongs, shall lose the official recognition of the party.

Detroit shall be the seat of the National Executive Committee for the ensuing term.

Philip Van Patten shall be the party secretary for the ensuing term.

Chicago will be the seat of the National Board of Supervision for the ensuing term.

REJECTED.

A press association and central publishing agency to be established in Cincinnati as soon as practicable, etc.

Our party will enter the Presidential campaign with candidates of our own.

The sections will vote upon each of the three following nominees: Caleb Pink and Osborn Ward, of New York, and Orrin A. Bishop, of Chicago, Ill., etc.

Our party will send no delegates to the proposed National Labor Convention at Chicago.

A special convention of the Socialistic Labor Party will be held at Chicago on or before July 4, 1880, for the purpose of publicly ratifying the nominations to be made by general vote.

Socialistic Labor Party.

NATIONAL BOARD OF SUPERVISION, NEW-ARK, NEW JERSEY.

All complaints, grievances and appeals, not adjustable by the Local, State or National Executive Committee, will be received and decided upon by this board.

Address, F. MEISELBACH, 616 Market st., Newark, N. J.

MEMBERSHIP.

Any person who acknowledges the Platform, Constitution and Resolutions of the National and State Conventions of the Socialistic Labor Party, and who renounces allegiance to all other political parties or organizations whose principles and requirements conflict with those of this party, may become a member.

In localities where no sections of the party exist, persons may join the party by sending their names and addresses, with dues for three months (30 cents), to Philip Van Patten, Secretary, Detroit, Mich. Cards of membership will then be issued, and as soon as ten such members (three-fourths of whom must be

or town, they will be notified, and will then organize themselves into a section by the election, by majority vote, of an organizer, a recording secretary, a corresponding secretary, a financial secretary, a treasurer and an auditing committee of two members.

SOCIALISTIC PAMPHLETS.—Better Times, by Dr. A. Douai, 5 cts; Lasalle's Open Letter, (translation), 10 cts; Coming Revolution, by L. B. Groenlund, 15 cts; Labor Catechism, by Osborn Ward, 25 cts; Capital, (extracts,) by Karl Marx, 20 cts; Does Socialism tend to Abolish Private Property? by John Ehmann, 5 cents; Why the State should Create a Bureau of Labor Statistics, by P. J. McGuire, 5 cts.

Address   PHILIP VAN PATTEN, P. O. Box 597, Detroit, Mich.

To Agents.

Agents are expected to settle their accounts by the first of each monh. Order about the number of REVIEWS you will need, and should any remain unsold, they can be returned.

THE Loranger Dramatic Club have issued handsome invitations for their second entertainment which takes place on Thursday evening, April 15, in Abstract Hall, when they will present the beautiful drama in two acts entitled "Among the Breakers."

THE wage-working slaves are fools to toil ten hours a day; fools to obey the dictates of the powers who control the avenues and sources of wealth. But how shall they escape? *First must come education to know; courage to act will soon follow.* —*The Trades.*

INJUSTICE and oppression are meant to be dangerous.—*Lord Hol-*

THE LABOR REVIEW.

Vol. 1.   No. 4.   DETROIT, MICH , APRIL, 1880.   Price Seven Cents.

DISCONTENT THE MOTHER OF PROGRESS.

Noble Discontent! forerunner of human liberties,
  With gratitude to thee we bow the head.
Memory doth bring back on wings of gladness and renown
  The good thou didst when naught would in thy stead.

As the bright and happy day dispels the gloom of night
  Dost thou the tyrannies of men remove;
And freedom's light pursues the darkness of despotic wrong,
  And freemen live in meek and humble love.

Thou art the Pandora's box of mankind's beatitudes;
  The rude corner-stone of progressive art;
The advance guard of much that is most noble, good and true,
  And rarely fail'st to take the better part.

No trivial irritation caused by a moment's pain
  Do we with grateful adoration praise,
But that soul-depressing feeling which justice long delayed
  Impels to action, colossal wrongs to raze.

Up from the dark ruins of autocratic sway
  Raised thou governments humane, good and strong,
Wherein doth rule the will of independent freemen,
  Whose brows with warning wrinkle at all wrong.

As the fresh and fragrant rose blooms from the thorny bud
  Contentment springs from thee in all its beauty,
And perfumes with aromas of prosperity and peace
  Those hardy men who dare perform their duty.

Vice—Its Cause.

A. P. RINTER.

Why should we enact laws to punish men for crimes when we ourselves are responsible for those crimes? "But," says the genteel member of society, "how am I responsible for the act of yon vile wretch whom the police have just caught in the act of stealing a loaf of bread?" As a member of society you *are* responsible; not individually, but jointly responsible. That man is hungry. He has a family, and they look to him for subsistence; his little children have turned their wan faces and sunken eyes to him and in piteous tones asked him for bread—*and he could not give it them!* He asked you for work and you told him you had none for him. He then appealed to you for bread for himself and his family, and you called him a *tramp*, and asked him why he was not at work. Was this not a little inconsistent? You refuse him work, and the next moment ask him why he is not at work. Not you as an individual; but society did, and you are a member of society. Victor Hugo says that English statistics prove four robberies out of five to have hunger for their immediate cause. The American Tract Society spent $40,000 last year in the printing and distribution of tracts. There were over 30,000 arrests in New York city for the theft of some article of food. In many cases the parties arrested, were proven to be honest people, who had been driven to this their first theft by actual starvation. Tracts may, in some instances, check vice; but we *know* bread would in thousands of cases *prevent* it.

You have done much for the poor man. You have unbound Liberty—or rather allowed Liberty to unbind herself—to a great extent. One by one she has cast aside the shackles man has to ask another, under penalty, how he shall worship; no man is thrown into prison for thinking and expressing what he thinks; you do not imprison a man for debt, and thus, because he is in trouble, use the strong arm of the law to increase his trouble. But there is one thing you have, to your own disgrace, allowed to remain unremedied, and this is the heaviest manacle on liberty to-day—that *one man is compelled to ask another man for the privilege of laboring;* and that other man has the privilege of refusing to let him, and thereby compel him to starve.

What are you Going to do About it?

P. M'NICHOLAS.

The greatest disadvantage of our present industrial system is the lack of time, and thereby of opportunity, afforded workingmen to study and inform themselves of the progress of events, and of the lessons they teach, for history continually repeats itself. This also is the case on matters that more immediately interest them personally and individually. The acquiring of a bare subsistance now takes from 10 to 14 hours a day. This is the cause of workingmen not being better posted on the construction of the government, and is likewise the reason they do not perceive its many defects. It was the manifest and emphatically declared intention of the founders of this republic that it should be a government of the people, by themselves, for themselves. A true democracy; not a government of the many by the few for selfish ends: the monarchical idea. A Chicago newspaper some time ago compared our system of government to a nest of sieves, the largest and coarsest representing the House of Representatives, who formulate the laws, turning them out in the rough, as it were;

where all superfluities were supposed to be removed; and lastly the final sieve was the President, who by this arrangement is supposed to embody the concentrated essence of the collective wisdom of the nation.

When we see that all measures for the amelioration of labor's condition are continually slighted, ignored and opposed by both national and state legislatures, or if passed in the House are opposed in the Senate and vetoed by the Governor,—as in Illinois, for instance, where the bills for the abolition of the truck system, the eight hour bill, the bill for the payment of wages weekly, etc., were systematically opposed by both the Senate and Executive,—when we see them, to use a phrase of Daniel O'Connell's, "drive a coach and six" right through the constitution of the United States, which guarantees to all citizens the right to bear arms, by passing laws making it a penal offense to do so, we are forced to the conclusion that senates and governors have outlived their usefulness and become obstructive and hurtful to the welfare of the people and *must go*, and be replaced by a system placing the veto power in the hands of the whole people, and not in the hands of one man or one class.

If the workingman had time to study what *true* republicanism is, he would recognize the fact that the President, with his appointing power, which gives him an influence no one man should have under a republican form of government, and his veto power, which presupposes him to know as much as two thirds of both houses of Congress, is a relic of kingly rule *which must go*. He would also notice the fact that the Senate is another unnecessary institution, being, like the English House of Lords, of which it is a copy, aristocratic in its very nature, checking, for the benefit of a class, at every

will, and therefore foreign to true democracy; and he would say, *that too, must go*. He would see that the only check on the House of Representatives should rest with the *sovereign people*, and not with one man or one class. And he would take steps to remove these obstacles to a true people's government. Now, he is only humbugged with the faint semblance of popular legislation, for we have no directly applicable control over our servants.

Who is to blame for all this? Of the many causes that have brought workingmen to their present servile condition, none stand out more prominently than the fact that workingmen have been criminally careless, and utterly neglectful of their duties. They have allowed their rights to be more and more encroached on by the monarchial, or one-man power, element.

And now, what is going to be done about it? That is a living question. The people need a concentration of all the electric forces of the universe into one irresistible galvanic shock, to awaken them from their lethargy, forcing them to see the immediate necessity of a practical answer to the above question.

The first and principal step is *education*. The education of the people must be accomplished through immediate practical measures bettering their condition by improving their environments. How is this to be done? Through *political action* lies the most direct road to the amelioration of the condition of wage-workers.

The present apathy of workingmen, in regard to political action for economic ends, is, to put it mildly, horrible. Trades Unions should be formed, not for the immediate purpose of strikes, but for the purpose of education, in order that at the proper time united political action may be had on these questions

men. And now let the reader study and compare the various platforms of the different parties, and choose the best and most suitable one for present needs as well as for future safety.

To Rich Men.

J F. BRAY.

The last twenty years have given birth to a multitude of rich men, but there are ten times as many poor men. Let the rich man and the poor man have a talk together, and compare notes.

Rich man, is it not a fact that you were once poor? Yes. And now, instead of receiving four or five hundred dollars a year as wages, for services rendered, you get four or five times as many thousands for doing nothing? Yes. Does your money grow, like a field of wheat? No, you know that somebody must earn every dollar of it. If somebody else earns it, and you get it, is not somebody cheated? Are not a multitude of men and women cheated, albeit "legally," in order that you may have five, twenty or fifty thousand dollars a year?

You hear a great many denunciations of communism and socialism, from pulpit and press. You don't know exactly what these terms mean, but are afraid they mean the taking back by the laborer of the wealth of which you have defrauded him by the "legal" rascality of interest, profit, stock-watering, speculative gambling, and other fraudulent inventions. But make your mind as easy as you can. Labor has no thoughts of plundering you, but is devising means to prevent any further plunder of itself by you.

You live in a palace. Did you work one single day in the erection of it, from foundation to chimney? Not one hour! Your palace is splendidly furnished. Did you make one piece of furniture, or one embellish-

done by men who work for wages, and who have to content themselves with the meanest dwellings, in crowded and filthy thoroughfares, deprived of every elevating and refining influence.

Ah! but you "paid them wages!" But where did you get the funds to pay them wages? Did you earn the money, as they do, by hard work? No, you got it by interest on money, by rents, by speculation, or by profits on the products of your factories, etc. You did not *earn* a dollar of it.

And how did you get your first start in "business," and escape from the ranks of the wage-workers? Perhaps you saved some money, borrowed some more, and then bought goods at a low price and sold them at a high price. You grew rich upon profits. Or you started a manufactory of some kind, hired men, paid a low price for the labor and sold the product at a high price, and grew rich out of the withheld wages of your employes. All your riches, except the moderate amount you originally saved, grew out of frauds upon the buyers of your goods, or the men who produced them. You were entitled to fair wages for your superintendence, but wages never make a man rich.

If you grew rich by "watering" railroad stock, you simply *forged* a representative of stock, and sold it or drew interest on it. It was a cheat and a fraud in either case. Rich man, whoever you are and wherever you stand, you are but as a monument representing the frauds, the rascalities, the wrongs, the tyrannies and the robberies of what is called "civilized society." Well might Christ denounce you. And yet it is not you who are to blame, but that social system which tolerates and encourages a wholesale plunder of the masses, through class divisions and the dependence of the

The fundamental truth of political economy and justice is, that labor creates all artificial wealth. It is only the man who works, or has worked, that has a rightful title to the artificial wealth of the world. If the workers do not possess it, then somebody has cheated them out of it. In former times they were cheated by force. In modern times they are cheated by concealed frauds. These frauds lie in interest and profits. They reach their arms everywhere and plunder labor everywhere. They are the agencies through which the wage-worker is robbed and reduced to hereditary servitude. There is no remedy apart from such industrial changes as will give labor the whole fruits of its toils, and entire control of its own destinies.

Now, then, rich man, it is charitably supposed that you have not realized that all your wealth was created by somebody else. But if you analyze your riches, and separate what *you* have created from that which *somebody else* has created, you will find that you have literally nothing you can justly call your own. It has come to you through inequitable social usages, and it is these fraudulent usages that we are endeavoring to supersede by others founded on justice to labor.

Rich man, you are now clamoring for a "strong government" and a large standing army. What for? Is the nation in peril from outsiders? Nothing of the kind. You are afraid of the insiders, the men whose toils

expect to consolidate a system of slavery more intolerable than that suffered by the negro, because it is applied to a higher grade of men and women. To do this effectively will require not only immense military forces in all directions, but also the demolition of the school-house, the newspaper and every instrumentality that leads to knowledge and progress, because these are fatal to tyranny everywhere.

You are undertaking a "big job." Before you can embrute a whole population you will have to destroy the enlightened "brutes" that now confront you on all your railroads, in your mines and manufacturing establishments and at the polls. Your cunningly devised parties are falling asunder. The people realize that they are frauds and implements of tyranny. A small mob is a small demon. A national mob, rising up in every locality, will be a terrible demon.

Now, rich man, you see how the matter stands. "As you measure to others it shall be measured to you again." The future will regard your position to-day as an excusable one, forced upon you by circumstances. If you appeal to force you will confess yourself a bandit, bent only on the plunder and poliation if the great world of labor. Whatever you may suffer the verdict of posterity will be, "served you right."

Labor is ready to meet you in friendly conference, and settle its demands on an equitable basis. It asks only for justice, and that jus-

upon wage-workers by your "strong government?" Does your "education, culture and refinement" end only in the production of a first-class idiot?

Rich men, don't be in a hurry with your armed police and bayonts. They sometimes hurt the wrong man. They are but wage-slaves, like the man they are to "put down." And they sometimes ask themselves why they should "put down" themselves, in common with their fathers and brothers? For the soldier who fights in support of a tyranny only puts a heavier halter on his own neck.

Come, then, rich man, and "let us reason together." It is better to look the whole issue squarely in the face. Circumstances make you a tyrant and the wage-worker a serf. Change those circumstances into such as will admit of neither tyranny nor servitude. Don't think of quenching the fire with blood, for blood calls for other blood; and whatever happens, compromises come in at the end, when there is but little to save. Let them rather come in at the beginning, when nothing has been lost. Not only social but political liberty is involved in this issue. You have everything to lose and the wage-worker everything to gain by a struggle of force. The conflict is too unequal for you to be thought of, unless riches have made you insane.

The Labor Review for March is to hand. It is published by the Co-operating Printers of Detroit, and is neatly printed, in magazine form. Economical reform and the moral and social advancement of working-men are the objects to which it is devoted. It is ably and fearlessly conducted, and a credit to the working-men of Detroit.—*The Exponent.*

Let reason, not prejudice, guide

THE CONVICT.

CHAPTER IV.

There was in the first quarter of this century a sort of pothouse at Montfermeil, near Paris, which no longer exists. It was kept by a couple of the name of Thenardier. A fragment of a vehicle blocked up the street in front of the inn. Under the axle-tree was festooned a heavy chain, suited for a convict Goliath. The centre of the chain hung rather close to the ground, and on the curve, as on the rope of a swing, two little girls were seated on this evening, in an exquisite embrace, one about two years and a half, the other about eighteen months; the younger being in the arms of the elder. An artfully tied handkerchief prevented them from falling, for a mother had seen this frightful chain, and said, "What a famous plaything for my children!" The two children, who were prettily dressed, and with some taste, were radiant; they looked like two roses among old iron; their eyes were a triumph, their healthy cheeks laughed; one had auburn hair, the other was a brunette; their innocent faces had a look of surprise; a flowering shrub a little distance off sent to passers-by a perfume which seemed to come from them; and the younger displayed her nudity with the chaste indecency of childhood. A few yards off, and seated in the inn door, the mother, a woman of no very pleasing appearance, but touching at this moment, was swinging them by the help of a long cord. While playing with her little ones, the mother sang, terribly out of tune, a romance, very celebrated at that day.

Her song and contemplation of her daughters prevented her hearing and seeing what took place in the street. Some one, however, had approached her, as she began the first couplets

heard a voice saying close to her ear: "You have two pretty children, Madame."

A woman was standing a few paces from her, who also had a child which she was carrying in her arms. She also carried a heavy bag. This woman's child was one of the most divine creatures possible to behold; she was a girl between two and three years of age, and could have vied with the two other little ones in the coquettishness of her dress. She had on a hood of fine linen, ribbons at her shoulders, and Valenciennes lace in her cap. Her raised petticoats displayed her white, dimpled, fine thigh: it was admirably pink and healthy, and her cheeks made one long to bite them. Nothing could be said of her eyes, except that they were very large, and that she had magnificent lashes, for she was asleep. She was sleeping with the absolute confidence peculiar to her age; a mother's arms are made of tenderness, and children sleep soundly in them. As for the mother, she looked grave and sorrowful, and was dressed like a work girl who was trying to become a country-woman again. She was young; was she pretty? perhaps so; but in this dress she did not appear so. Her hair, a light lock of which peeped out, seemed very thick, but was completely hidden beneath a nun's hood. Laughter displays fine teeth, when a person happens to possess them; but she did not laugh. Her eyes looked as if they had not been dry for a long time; she had a fatigued and rather sickly air, and she looked at the child sleeping in her arms in the manner peculiar to a mother who has suckled her babe. A large blue handkerchief, like those served out to invalids, folded like a shawl, clumsily hid her shape. Her hands were rough and covered with red spots, and her fore-finger was hardened and torn by the needle. She had on a brown cloth cloak, a woman's name was Fantine. Fantine could hardly read, and could not write. She had commited a fault, but the foundation of her nature, was modesty and virtue. She felt vaguely that she was on the eve of falling into distress, and gliding into worse. She needed courage, and she had it. The idea occurred to her of returning to her native town M. sur M. There some might know her, and give her work; but she must hide her fault. And she vaguely glimpsed at the possible separation, but she formed her resolution. Fantine, as we shall see, possessed the stern bravery of life. She sold all she possessed, which brought her in 200 francs; and when she had paid her little debts, she had only about 80 francs left. At the age of two-and-twenty, on a fine spring morning, she left Paris, carrying her child on her back. Any one who had seen them pass would have felt pity for them; the woman had nothing in the world but her child, and the child had nothing but her mother in the world.

At midday, after resting herself now and then, Fantine found herself at Montfermeil. As she passed the inn, the two little girls in their monster swing had dazzled her, and she stopped before this vision of joy. These two little creatures were evidently happy. She looked at them and admired them with such tenderness, that she could not refrain from saying:

"You have two pretty children, Madame."

The most ferocious creatures are disarmed by a caress given to their little ones. The mother raised her head, thanked her, and bade her sit down on the door bench. The two women began talking.

"My name is Madame Thenardier," the mother of the little ones said; "we keep this inn."

Madame Thenardier was a red-

was still young, scarce thirty. If she had been standing, instead of sitting, perhaps her colossal proportions, fitting for a show, would have at once startled the traveler, destroyed her confidence, and prevented what we have to record. A person sitting down instead of standing up—destinies hang on this.

The woman told her story with some modification. She was a work girl; her husband was dead; she could get no work in Paris, and was going to seek it elsewhere, in her native town. She had left Paris that very morning on foot; the little one had walked a little, but not much, for she was so young, and she had been obliged to carry her, and the darling had gone to sleep—and as she said this she gave her daughter a passionate kiss which awoke her. The babe opened her eyes, large blue eyes like her mother's. The child began laughing, and, though its mother had to check it, slipped down to the ground with the undauntable energy of a little creature wishing to run. All at once she noticed the other two children in their swing, stopped short, and put out her tongue as a sign of admiration. Mother Thenardier unfastened her children, took them out of the swing, and said:

"Play about all three."

Iu a minute the little Thenardiers were playing with the new comer at making holes in the ground, which was an immense pleasure. The stranger child was very merry; the goodness of the mother is written in the gaiety of the baby. She had picked up a piece of wood which she used as a spade, and was energetically digging a grave large enough for a fly. The two went on talking.

"What's the name of your bantling?"

"Cosette."

"What is her age?"

"Going on for three."

one another," Mother Thenardier exclaimed; "why, they might be taken for three sisters."

The word was probably the spark which the other mother had been waiting for; she seized the speaker's hand, looked at her fixedly, and said: "Will you take charge of my child for me?"

The woman gave one of those starts of surprise which are neither assent nor refusal. Fantine continued:

"Look ye, I cannot take the child with me to my town, for when a woman has a baby, it is a hard matter for her to get a situation. People are so foolish in our part. It was Heaven that made me pass in front of your inn; when I saw your little ones so pretty, so clean, so happy, it gave me a turn, I said to myself, 'She is a kind mother.' It is so; they will be three sisters. Then I shall not be long before I come back. Will you take care of my child?"

"We will see," said Mother Thenardier.

"I would pay six francs a month."

Here a man's voice cried from the back of the tap-room:

"Can't be done under seven, and six months paid in advance."

"I will pay it," said the mother.

"And seventeen francs in addition for extra expenses," the man's voice continued.

"I will pay it, I will pay it," the mother said; "I have eighty francs, and shall have enough left to get home on foot. I shall earn money there, and as soon as I have a little I will come and fetch my darling."

The man's voice continued: "Has the little one a stock of clothing?"

"It is my husband," said Mother Thenardier.

"Of course she has clothes, a dozen of everything, and silk frocks like a lady."

"They must be handed over," the

"Of course they must," said the mother; "it would be funny if I left my child naked."

The master's face appeared. "All right," he said.

The bargain was concluded, the mother spent the night at the inn, paid her money and left her child, with the intention of returning soon. A neighbor's wife saw the mother going away, and went home saying: "I have just seen a woman crying in the street as if her heart was broken."

When Cozette's mother had gone, the man said to his wife: "That money will meet my note for 110 francs, which falls due to-morrow. It would have been protested, and I should have had a bailiff put in. You set a famous mouse-trap with your brats."

"Without suspecting it," said the woman.

The captured mouse was a very small one, but the cat is pleased with a thin mouse. Who were the Thenardiers?

To be continued.

Communism.

Detroit people are now being instructed upon the subject of "Communism," by the Rev. P. B. Morgan. Instructed, did we say? We meant *talked to.* Unfortunately the reverend gentleman neglected to explain or even fairly mention the principles of communism, but wandered off into a recitation of the horrible events which occurred in Paris when the Commune was crushed. This

The reverend lecturer said the excesses committed in Paris demonstrated sufficiently the evils of communism. We would call the Doctor's attention to the millions of murders and most horrible crimes perpetrated in the name of Christianity—outrages by the side of which those of an hundred revolutions such as that of Paris sink into insignificance. Because crimes were sanctioned by the Church, does it follow that Christianity is bad in principle?

Rev. Morgan admits that communism is the outgrowth of oppression and tyranny; yet in the next breath he informs us that it is all that is selfish and terrible! We noticed one peculiarity in the Doctor's remarks (which, by the way, is always noticeable in the utterances of those who are but half-informed upon a subject), namely, his inconsistency—one moment lauding the real principles of communism, and the next denouncing the thing itself in the bitterest terms.

The gentleman forgets the motto of the French communists—"Liberty, Equality and Fraternity." "Love thy neighbor as thyself" is a basic principle of communism.

"Do unto others as you would have others do unto you" is written upon the heart of every communist. True, many excesses occurred during the French Revolutions; but did the Doctor ever hear of a war in which nobody was killed? Were men ever redeemed from slavery and oppression except by bloody revolution?

THE LABOR REVIEW.

DETROIT, MICH., APRIL, 1880.

TERMS OF SUBSCRIPTION.

One year, in advance, - - 75 cents
Six months, in advance, - - 40 cents
Three months, in advance, - 20 cents
Single copies, - - - - 7 cents

☞ Terms to Agents, four cents per copy. Agents must make returns by the first of each month, and also stating how many copies are needed.

☞ When a subscription has expired, the subscriber will be notified, and if he does not renew before the next number is issued, his name will be dropped from the list. Address,

CO-OPERATING PRINTERS,
121 Porter street, Detroit, Mich.

To Agents.

No copies of the May Review will be sent any Agent that does not remit, by the first of May, in full for the March and April numbers. As will be seen under head of "Terms," Agents are supplied the Review at four cents a copy.

The Month's Review.

The strike of the cigar-makers of Cincinnati against signing a pledge that they should not belong to their Union, has resulted in a victory for the men. Of over 1,000 men on strike, only four deserted the Union, and now these four have been discharged.

We have never seen recorded a victory so complete as that of the piano-makers of New York city. The manufacturers locked their men out for assisting each other when on strike, and the men resolved not to resume work until a ten per cent. advance had been conceded. With orders for pianos coming in, and no workmen to be found willing to fill the places of the locked-out men; and with the fact that piano manufacturers in other cities had voluntarily advanced their workmen's

ner" made by their employes too strong to be broken, and so they acceded to the request of the men. In this connection we record the offer made to the manufacturers by a "philanthropic" woman, the head of a "mission," to supply 5,000 Chinamen, skilled, industrious and frugal, "who would not be particular whether they labored eight, ten or twelve hours, and who would work very cheap." The offer was declined.

Congressman Newbury, of this district, lately presented to the House of Representatives, a petition signed by nearly 1,000 Detroit workingmen, for the enforcement of the eight hour law now on the statute books.

Trouble is brewing in some of the Louisiana parishes. The negro laborers, finding the cost of living increased, are agitating for higher wages. But their unorganized condition, and general ignorance, give little hope of any pronounced success. The Governor of the State has already called out the militia to "put them down."

Owing to the disregard by the proprietors of the mills in Cohoes, N. Y., of their promise not to discharge those who were prominent in the late strike, the men are again out. Agents are scouring Canada for help, and such a large number of French Canadians have arrived that the strike is virtually over.

In most of the cities of the United States, the past two months, carpenters have received an average advance of 25 per cent.

Disbanded labor unions that have fallen apart during the years of depression, are being reorganized everywhere.

The cigar packers of Cincinnati are considering the advisability of joining the cigar-makers union.

Nearly all the leading railroads in the country have restored the wages of their employes to the figures of

Successful strikes have occurred among the safe-makers of Cincinnati, O.; the carpenters of Pittsburg, Pa.; the cabinet-makers of Piqua, O.; the New York longshoremen; and in several other places. The failures have been few and far between.

Wages in England are on the up-grade. The iron-workers of Stockton-on-Tees have received an advance, other places are demanding it, and as soon as the surplus labor is absorbed a general advance is certain. In Preston, an agreement has been entered into by the manufacturers and the spinners' union whereby an advance of 5 per cent. is given now, and another like advance will be made in June.

Russian nihilism has scored its first victory. The "powers that be" are so thoroughly alarmed that great reforms have been promised. This is a virtual acknowledgment that the demands of the Nihilists are just. On the death of the Czarina and the abdication of the Czar, both of which are not far distant, a more enlightened and humane policy will, it is to be hoped, govern their rulers. But there, as here, in the end monarchy and aristocracy will be replaced by a true democracy.

In Germany the Socialistic movement is the labor movement. Not only through trades unions, but by a political union, are the workers striving for economic freedom; and it is no wonder that Socialism, offering the enslaved and toiling masses freedom. from degradation and pov-

Notes by the Way.

MEN grow weaker by every consent to wrong; stronger by every resistance to wrong.

DETROIT Typographical Union elected the following officers at their regular April meeting:

President—Lyman A. Brant.
Vice President—Frank J. C. Ellis.
Rec. Secretary—Chas. O. Brice.
Cor. Secretary—J. A. Labadie.
Fin. Secretary—Rulif Duryea.
Treasurer—F. B. Eagan.

EDITOR McDonnell and laborer Menton have been released from their imprisonment, their terms having expired. On the day of their release the wage-workers of Paterson gave them a grand ovation, followed by a banquet.

Some of our friends tell us we are too radical in our views of the labor question. We believe we are right, and if we are right we cannot be too radical. If we were in the wrong we could not be too conservative. Read the articles carefully which appear in THE REVIEW, and we are of the opinion that our readers will not long think us " too radical."

THE rules enforced in the Jackson State Prison have been adopted by the foreman of the *Post and Tribune* job rooms. Of course, its all right. The men like such rules; because, you see, if they didn't they would go to work and form a co-operative association, work for themselves, take all the profits and make their own rules.

THE Crispins of Detroit have is-

OCCUPYING the last two pages of this number of THE REVIEW will be found an excellent tract on "The Paris Commune." The ignorance of the people concerning the aims and objects of the much-slandered Paris Commune, renders this contribution particularly valuable; and this fact leads us to offer "The Paris Commune," in tract form, at 30 cts. per hundred, or ten for 5 cts.

THE Workingmen's Club Room has been removed to the corner of Randolph and Lafayette sts. They have now two rooms, one used as a dining and reading room, and the other as a kitchen. A good breakfast, dinner or supper is served for ten cents. Workingmen should patronize the Club Room, and do all in their power to help establish on a sound financial basis this institution.

F. H. BURGESS, editor and publisher of The Truthteller, of this city, has started a department in his paper, devoted to interests of working men and women. A number of prominent labor advocates have promised him their aid. We trust the workingmen of Detroit will show their appreciation of his good will by giving him all the material support they can. Copies of The Truthteller can be found at the Workingmen's Club Room, corner of Randolph and Lafayette streets.

THE Cincinnati Exponant, organ of the Trades and Labor Assembly of that city, has budded out into a really first-class paper for working-men. And we cannot but note the differance in favor of the labor papers of to-day, compared with those of a dozen years ago. The principles of political economy, as regards the law of wages, the law of population and its effect on wages, the law of prices in relation to the medium of exchange, etc., are now becoming as familiar to working-men as they were then unfamiliar.

Surely the time can not be far distant when wage-workers will see the necessity of restricting the now almost irresponsible power of corporations and individuals in industrial affairs, in order that they may be truly free to do as they please in political affairs.

"LABOR is fighting its battles, and victory is perching on its banners." Very true; but for how long? Don't let us hurrah too loud. This boom will not last always. Our present planness production and unjust system of distribution will inevitably cause in the near future a panic and crash. Then where will the workingman be? Would it not be wise to look around and see if we can not discover some way whereby both production and distribution could be controlled in the interest of the producers, and so avoid these periodic crashes?

THE special privileges of kings, aristocracies and churches have been the bane of the world in all times. In the United States these have been abrogated only in name. The man of money is distinguished from the man of labor. He is the representative of the king, the aristocrat and the church. He grows fat through the spoliation of labor by profit and usury, and strong through the legislation which a servile and dependent labor permits him to control. He is an alien from Christianity in spirit and practice. The brotherhood of humanity is to him a myth or a pious fraud.—From "God and Man a Unity."

SUBSCRIBERS and agents will bear in mind that the publishers of THE REVIEW are wage workers, and do the work on it after their regular working hours and cannot afford to furnish it free. We therefore will be compelled to discontinue the magazine after subscriptions have expired.

The Council of Trades and Labor Unions.

Nine unions have already adopted the new constitution and sent delegates to the Council, which now meets every Monday evening at 65 Michigan avenue. Permanent officers elected April 12 as follows:

President—F. B. Egan, printer.
Vice President—R. D. Howe, cooper.
Recording Secretary—E. W. Simpson, carpenter.
Financial Secretary—C. O. Bryce, printer
Corresponding Secretary and Statistician—J. A. Labadie, printer.
Treasurer—A. Stuermer, cigarmaker.
Trustees—John Strigel, shoemaker; E. Wesselhoft, cigarmaker; R. B. Hall, carpenter.
Sergeant-at-Arms—B. Reilly, ship carpenter.

Vigorous steps will be taken to strengthen all present labor unions and establish new ones in trades now unorganized, for which a committee on organization was appointed. We predict that in less than three months 20 unions will be represented in the Council; and then confidence in their power to legislate both economically and politically will begin to pervade the minds of the wage workers of Detroit.

Longheaded men are interested in the success of the Council. No rash steps will be undertaken, and no union advised to strike before all peaceable means to gain their rights have been exhausted, and ample preparations made for every emergency likely to arise in striking.

We expect good results in the event of a strike from the enforcement of the third section of the con-

SOCIALISTIC LABOR PARTY

Summary of Proceedings of the Nat. Ex. Committee.

FURNISHED BY THE SECRETARY, PHILIP VAN PATTEN.

NATIONAL EXECUTIVE COMMITTEE.

P. O. Christiansen............Antoine st.
Charles Erb............579 Dequinde st.
Judson Grenell............116 Howard st.
Gustav Herzig............29 Napoleon st.
Philip Van Patten.........P. O. Box 597
E. W. Simpson...........90 Wilkins st.
Henry Walters...........407 Macomb st.

The Chicago Labor Convention.

The propositions of the National Executive Committee to the Sections are about as as follows:

1. Each State in which Socialists have an organization will send at least one delegate; but they are not restricted to that number. It would be a good plan for each State to send as many delegates as they have electoral votes.

2. Delegates must have been members of the party, for at least one year.

3. States unable to send their own delegates will transmit their credentials in blank to the National Executive Committee, by whom proper proxies will be furnished from among the Sections of Chicago and other neighboring cities.

The delegates will promise the support and votes of Socialists for the candidates nominated by the convention, under the following conditions:

1. The platform must declare such principles and contain such de-

do not represent or advocate principles hostile to Socialism.

3. The platform and candidates chosen by the Conveniion must be submitted to a ratification vote of all Sections of the party, before support can be positively promised.

———o———

Amendments to the Constitution.

The Sections are called upon to vote for or against the following amendments to the constitution:

III. EXECUTIVE COMMITTEES.

The National Executive Committee, Par. b, 3d District, to include the whole of Illinois and Iowa.   Fourth District to include the State of Louisiana and all the other Southwestern States.

SECTION REGULATIONS.

Par. 10 to be amended by the addition of the following words after "to the Nat. Executive Committee," "which sum shall be held by the Section Treasurer in trust for the Nat. Executive Committee (or State Executive committee where such exists), and shall not be paid out by him for any local purposes, the Section having no jurisdiction over such money other than to assure its proper payment to the party authorities as required by the constitution."

———o———

Official Notice.

"The Bulletin of the Social Labor Movement" having been merged into "The Labor Review," all agents and subscribers indebted to us on account of the "Bulletin" will please forward at once to the undersigned all amounts due. We trust that delinquent agents will need no further notice, but will settle up immediately.

PHILIP VAN PATTEN, Sec'y,
For Nat. Ex. Com.
P. O· Box 597.   Detroit, Mich.

———o———

The Presidential Campaign.

In consideration of the fact that the Sections have resolved almost unanimously to nominate no independent Presidential candidates of our own, but to participate in the campaign by supporting the nominees of the Labor Convention at Chicago(on June 9th), provided the said Convention shall act in an honorable and independent manner, such as our members can endorse; and since the Sections generally express their desire to have delegates, therefore we have submitted for your decision a number of propositions, to be voted upon at once. The result must be communicated to our Committees on or before May 10th, next ensuing, showing the exact number of votes cast for and against each proposition. (Sections in large cities, in which two or more branches exist, shall take the vote of the branches separately, but report to us the sum total in the affirmative and negative for the entire Section.)

PHILIP VAN PATTEN, Sec'y.
For Nat. Ex. Com.

[All Sections having been provided with these propositions, it is unnecessary to repeat them here.]

———o———

Financial Report of the Executive Committee for March.

RECEIPTS.

Philadelphia Section, dues			$7 35
James Poppers,Chicago,pamphlets.			10
Milwaukee Section, dues			2 15
San Francisco, Cal.,Ed,"Rosebud,"			09
Davenport (Ia.,) Section, dues.			90
Boston Section, dues			2 00
Cincinnati Section, dues			2 00
P. C. Christiansen,Detroit,pamphlets			25
Cleveland Section, dues			5 75
Baltimore " "			4 80
San Francisco Section, dues.......			7 75
Boston do do			2 00
New Orleans do do			6 30
Hoboken do do			2 00
New Haven do do			9 35
Detroit do do			9 35
St. Joseph do do			3 15
New York do do			43 15
Union Hill, N. J., do			3 20
Jersey City Heights, do			2 65

$114.59

BULLETIN RECEIPTS.

W. F. Schmidt, Philadelphia, $2.00; G. Lizius, Indianapolis, 85c; C. T. Neidert, Newark, $1.80; Jno. P. Hutson, Baltimore, 50c; N. A. Geissler, NewOrleans, $1.20; J. E. Damerid, Jersey City, 48c; H. Moorman, Louisville; $1.   Total, 7.33.

EXPENDITURES.

Alleghany Section, for expenses of Convention	$45 00
Board of Supervision, for current expenses	2 00
C. E. Collenburg, translating and revising records of Convention,etc	3 69
Current expenses, postage, etc....	9 54
Salary of Secretary, five weeks	60 00

THE PARIS COMMUNE.

Address of Philip Van Patten at Workmen's Hall, Detroit, Mich., March 1880.

Mr. Chairman and Fellow-Workingmen.

We have assembled this afternoon for the purpose of celebrating the anniversary of a day whose memory is dear to all radicals and friends of struggling labor throughout the world—the Eighteenth of March. That day witnessed the uprising in Germany in 1848, and the no less eventful one of 1871 in Paris. It is more especially to commemorate this latter occasion that we have gathered here, for the objects of the Paris Commune were more important, the principles more radical, and the struggle more heroic. Owing to the lies of the capitalistic press and cowardice of modern historians, we are compelled to defend the martyrs of Paris while denouncing their murderers, so that our task is a double one. So much ignorance prevails among Americans concerning the intentions and official actions of the Commune, that we must ask your indulgence to recite briefly some of the historical facts.

For more than a century there had been a movement throughout France in favor of establishing a true republic. Often had the goal been nearly reached, when traitors, monarchists and cowards forced France back into despotism. But at the close of the Franco-Prussian war, when the ambitious Napoleon 3d (Napoleon the Little) was a prisoner and France was without a government, the republicans determined to seize the opportunity and forever liberate France from monarchy. Paris was, as usual, first to take the initiative. No sooner had the city been surrendered to the Prussians, and hostilities ceased, than the citizens began thinking of the future, and considering how they should be governed. The masses desired a republican form of government, and naturally proposed to commence by making Paris, for the first time, a self-governing city—that is, a *commonwealth*,

for the French word Commune means nothing else. For the benefit of ignorant Americans, I will merely remind them that every township or parish in France was then and is now called, officially, a commune; for the people there elect their own mayor, clerks, etc. Paris desired also to be a commonwealth, with local self-government. Hitherto it had been ruled by men appointed by the empire; and when the empire fell, the rural national assembly sought to govern it. For generations the people of France had found themselves, in their ardent struggle for freedom, dragged back and crushed down by the ignorance and prejudice of the country people, ruled by landlords and priests. The empire was one long struggle of Paris with the peasants. For the last 20 years the intelligence and spirit of Paris had writhed under the yoke, but the workmen never acknowledged the tyrant. The opportunity offered by his fall was too valuable to be lost.

But the Prussians who knew the consequences likely to follow if Paris should once feel herself at liberty, stipulated that the city should continue to be held down by the national assembly, for they feared Paris more than all the armies of Napoleon. The assembly hastened to comply with the instructions, but they found an indignant people armed to resist them; a people outraged and alarmed by the reckless policy of the assembly and their avowed hostility to Paris. The workingmen resolved to rally to the rescue. Fortunately the national guard, 180,000 in number, had been permitted to retain their arms. They seized the cannon and placed themselves on the defensive. In 24 hours the workmen were masters of Paris. And on March 18th, the committee of delegates proclaimed at the Hotel de Ville that Paris was at last a commonwealth—a commune! The great city was filled with joy! The national guards and citizens of all classes welcomed the proclamation with cheers, songs, and salvos of artillery.

Meanwhile the self-appointed government of the national defense, composed of the old politicians and creatures of the empire, finding their proclamation disregarded and their authority denied, fled to Versailles, and appealed to the national assembly. The appeal was not in vain. The entire army of the Line was marshaled to the attack, and Paris found herself again besieged. The Prussian army on one side formed an impassable barrier. The French army completed the circuit, and the city was doomed. Notwithstanding the threatened attack, a general municipal election had been held, and Paris had a government of her own choosing. The election was fully announced, and was as fair and just an expression of the popular will as was ever an election in Detroit.

Those traducers in America (and I do not except the "Hon." E. B. Washburne) who assert that Paris was at the mercy of a mob of drunken roughs, are guilty of the most outrageous falsehoods; whether through ignorance or malice, or both, I do not choose to say. The central committee of the Commune was composed of men prominent for their ability and learning, fully equal in intelligence to Mr. Washburne himself, and morally his superior. It has been admitted by capitalistic authorities, including our own Gen. Sheridan, who was present, that until the army of the Line had stormed Paris, there was better order and less crime than was ever before known in that great city.

It is true that the commonwealth of Paris intended to inaugurate greater Social Reforms than was pleasing to the aristocracy and the capitalists. Those men knew that political liberty without industrial freedom is but an empty phrase. Herein lay the secret of the whole conflict. The national assembly was willing, if necessary, to establish a middle-class Republic; something like that in America, but proposed to perpetuate industrial oligarchy and use the political forms of a Republic in such a way as to delude the masses and plunder them with safety. This was the truth, and nothing but the truth.

The siege lasted many weeks, until at last, deserted by the cowardly bourgeois who had first shouted the loudest, the workmen saw that their efforts were in vain. The outlying forts were all captured and their guns turned against the city. The soldiers of the Line swarmed into the streets shooting indiscriminately men, women and children, storming the barricades and sweeping everything before them! Frenchmen shooting Frenchmen! Workingmen in uniform killing workmen in blouses, and all to uphold capitalistic rule. No mercy was shown, and the slaughter was horrible! Over 30,000 men, women and children were murdered in cold blood, and all rules of civilized warfare were ignored! Can it be wondered at that the workmen, who knew they were doomed to die, who saw that all the Powers of Europe were against them, and their fate inevitable, became desperate as wolves at bay, and were transformed into furies? It is true they burned public buildings, but not until all hope was lost. It is true that they killed an Archbishop, but not until after the Versailles government had refused to exchange prisoners, and had shot the captured leaders of the Commune without trial, in cold blood. The Archbishop had been held as a hostage, but the Versaillais having refused the exchange of prisoners, were themselves his murderers! Perhaps there was haste, and misunderstanding; and the killing of the Archbishop might have been avoided. It could be justified only as a war-measure, for the principles of the Commune call for no murder of priests any more than of the most harmless infants. Whether or not the Archbishop was unjustly killed, concerns not in the least the principles for which the workmen of Paris fought. The death of Archbishop Darboy could not justify the destruction of a people's liberties!

It is true the Column Vendome was pulled down. It deserved to be. It was a monument to glorify murder, conquest and one-man power, and was a standing disgrace to Paris.

We admit that many acts were committed by the dying heroes of the Commune which might have been left undone; but their mistakes are as nothing compared to the horrible crime perpetrated against them by the capitalistic assassins. Those patriots have given up their lives in defence of their principles, and History will some day vindicate them.

Let us prove by our actions that the lesson has not been in vain. Let us show our reverence for their glorious effort by manfully striving to spread the true principles which they died to maintain. And let us hope that when the workmen of America have their Eighteenth of March, there will be sufficient intelligence, honor and courage in our people, to make this Republic what it was intended to be.

THE LABOR REVIEW.

VOL. 1.   No. 5.   DETROIT, MICH , MAY, 1880.   PRICE SEVEN CENTS.

THE LABOR REVIEW.

TERMS OF SUBSCRIPTION.

One year, in advance, - - 75 cents
Six months, in advance, - - 40 cents
Three months, in advance, - 20 cents
Single copies, - - - - 7 cents

☞ Terms to Agents, four cents per copy. Agents must make returns by the first of each month, and also stating how many copies are needed.

☞ When a subscription has [expired, the subscriber will be notified, and if he does not renew before the next number is issued, his name will be dropped from the list. Address,

CO-OPERATING PRINTERS,
121 Porter street, Detroit, Mich.

What Socialism Means.

One of the missions of Socialism is to stop the wastes of the world.

Socialism means order and system in place of disorder and want of system.

It means a stopping of the ruinous waste that characterizes this system of disorder.

It means the conversion of an army of non-producers into an army of producers.

It means more workers and less work for each.

It means that, as far as possible, machinery shall perform the labor of the world.

It means that all labor-saving machinery shall be owned by the people as a whole, and that the production of that machinery shall be used for the good of the people as a whole.

It means death to politics as a business.

It means that voting shall not be a sham, and that representation shall

It means no granting of monopolies to persons or companies.

It means that all sources of wealth shall be preserved and developed by the people for the people.

It means that money shall be the people's servant, and not the people's master.

It means the total extinction of that class of men called millionaires.

It means an abolition of that class called tramps.

It means an abolition of that class called poor men.

It means an extinction of that class called rich men.

It means no breathing room for idle men.

It means the right men in the right place.

It means that the rights of the individual are paramount to every other consideration.

It means that the world is man's country, and that all men are his brethren.

It means an end to war and all its horrors; and in its place, peace with all its blessings.

It means the entire abolition of all capitalists.

It means that the people as a whole shall be the only capitalist.

It means that the time of all men is of equal value.

It means that no man shall own an acre of land, but the people as a whole shall own all the land.

It means that the cultivation of the land is the title to its occupancy.

It means that all small farms will pass away, and that the people will live in palaces and farm immense domains on the basis of co-operation.

the opportunity to make the best of himself.

It means that there is no knowledge, scientific or otherwise, that every man cannot acquire, if he has the requisite mental ability and determination.

It means that all children are born equal, and shall have equal chances in life.

It means that all children shall have the very best physical, mental and moral culture.

It means that no child can be fatherless or motherless, for every man will be to it as a father, and every woman will be to it as a mother.

It means that every sick person shall have the best care and attention that humanity can give and medical science devise.

It means the liberation of women from household drudgeries.

It means that women in all phases of life shall have equal rights and opportunities with men.

It means the very best conditions and life for every man, woman and child.

It means carrying into practice the principles of the Declaration of Independence.

Socialism means Evolution and Revolution: for evolution exists not only in the slow and silent, though irresistible, forces of nature, but also in its sudden changes and occasional catastrophes.

LIZZIE DENTON SEYBOLD.

The Proper Aim of Politics.

Our industrial interests are the ones on which all others are based. They are our nearest and most important ones, and through proper legislation alone can we ever have them correctly regulated.

That is politics, properly so called, and not the mere scheming for place now honored by that name. Politics is our public business, as citizens of a great republic, to be at-tended to by ourselves, and no longer left to a few unscrupulous schemers. It is worthy our closest attention,.and must receive it. If we paid as little attention to our private business as we have done to our public affairs, we should soon find ourselves in the poor-house. P.

Trades Unions and Strikes.

[Remarks of Comrade W. G. H. Smart, before the Lyceum in the City Hall, West Newton, Mass. Subject of debate: "Resolved, That strikes are injurious to the laboring classes."]

The question whether strikes are injurious to the laboring classes is very similar in character to the question whether wars are injurious to civilized nations. Neither is in itself a question worth discussing. Under the present conditions of civilization—the conflict of interests between nations—*wars are inevitable*. They are the natural consequences of opposing interests. So of strikes. Under the present conflict of interests between different classes of society—using the terms laborers and capitalists as representing those classes—*strikes are inevitable*. Wars can only cease by the removal of conditions that cause wars. Strikes can only cease by the removal of the conditions that cause strikes. The conflict of interests between nations must be replaced by unity of interests between nations; that is, by the absorption of nations into one broad nationality of civilized humanity.

The conflict of interests between classes must be replaced by unity of interests between classes; that is, by the absorption of classes into one comprehensive class—the whole people.

That is the idea of the Declaration of Independence; and of the Constitution of the United States. It is the American idea of democracy. The same line that separates the classes called laborers and capitalists separates the classes known as the rich and the poor. That line must be obliterated.

The capitalists are capitalists by virtue of their riches.

The laborers are laborers by virtue of their poverty.

The rich are not rich because of natural superiority, or any other good quality.

The poor are not poor because of natural inferiority, or any other bad quality.

"We hold this truth to be self-evident: *That all men are created equal.*"

The Bible says truly: "The curse of the poor is their poverty." Which means this, if it means anything: The poor are poor because they are poor.

The poor can only live by labor. They cannot labor without the means of labor.

This becomes more and more true as population increases, as civilization advances, and as the natural resources and all other means of labor become monopolized by the rich.

The rich can live without labor. They can, if need be, live upon their riches; or they can live upon the labor of the poor by loaning to them the means of labor and exacting tribute therefor (the Bible name for tribute is "Usury"); or they can attain the same end in several other ways, and in all ways making slaves of the poor; increasing their own riches and bestowing upon the poor only the barest means of subsistence. The rich have the mastery over the poor, which becomes more and more oppressive as the superabundance of labor and the consequent competition between the laborers for the use of the means of labor increases.

Every rich man sees it to his interest to give back as little as possible to the poor man in return for his labor.

And every poor man sees it to be his interest to obtain as much for his labor as he possibly can. He knows that he is robbed by the rich continually, and the fear of hunger only compels him to submit.

Therefore, There is a conflict of interests between the rich and the poor; between the laborers and the capitalists.

Therefore, also: Strikes.

Strikes are the inevitable consequences of the self-evident conflict between capital and labor as these two factors of producing and distributing wealth are related under our present laws.

The question whether strikes, in the sense intended in the question before us, are injurious to the laboring classes or not, is really wholly inconsequential.

Injurious or not, like wars, they have got to be; or, at least they have got to be until some better means of defence and resistance present themselves to the best judgment of the laboring classes. Every proposition looking to that end which is proposed or commended by their oppressors the capitalists, or the parasites of their oppressors, the educated classes, the press, the clergy, etc., workingmen should and do look upon at least with distrust.

The rich, believing as they do, that the means by which they take advantage of the poverty of the poor is just and righteous because it is lawful (just as the slaveholders thought with regard to slavery), cannot be expected to approve of any means of helping the poor that would injure themselves; and, as the laborer cannot get any more for his labor without the capitalist getting less than he is obliged to accept, the laborer is a fool who listens to the advice of the capitalist in such matters.

But, to return to the question: "Are strikes injurious to the laboring classes?" I answer: In a local, narrow and limited sense, *Yes*, perhaps. In a wider and more general sense, *No*. And in a still wider and far more important sense, *Yes*, again.

1. Viewing the subject in the narrow, pecuniary sense of the last report of the Massachusetts Bureau of Statistics of Labor; that is, averaging all the strikes that occur in a series of years; ascertaining what was the loss in wages and contributions for that average one during the continuance of the strike, and all other losses to the strikers on account of it; multiplying that by the number of strikes, and thus getting the aggregate pecuniary loss to a limited number of laborers for the whole of them; then, comparing this total with the aggregate gain to this same limited number of laborers directly concerned in the strikes through increase of their wages only —and confining this estimate to a limited period of time —possibly a loss might be proven, although I think it doubtful.

2. But, taking the wider and more general sense in which I have given the answer, *No !* I think the advantages obtained by the laboring classes through "strikes," immeasurably exceed the disadvantages.

Even pecuniarily there has been a great gain; a gain that no statistics can show or dispute, and that cannot be estimated. A gain in many ways: A gradual rise in wages and reduction of the hours of labor from the first strike—a gain not produced by other causes, as it has shown itself in those branches of labor in which the strikes have occurred, and only indirectly and subsequently in other industries in consequence of these strikes. A rise in wages, also, especially in those sections where strikes were resorted to; and, be it noticed, that this increase of wages everywhere has not been confined to the actual strikers, but has been general wherever the same industries were carried on; and not only in one country only, but in all countries. Moreover, the general effect has been to advance wages of all kinds of labor everywhere.

So much for the pecuniary gain. But a still greater gain has arisen, in my opinion, from the increased power afforded to the laboring classes through the organization into trades unions that become necessary to institute and maintain strikes.

Armies and navies are necessary as a means of carrying on war and preparing for war, and sometimes of preventing war. But if we had no wars we should have no armies or navies.

So, trades unions are the necessary machinery of strikes, and preparing for and some times preventing strikes. But if we had *no strikes;* that is, if strikes had not become necessary, there would be *no trades-unions.*

Now, who will venture to say that trades-unions have not been of far more value to the laboring classes than they have been injurious? I must not stop to even mention the benefits arising from trades-unions especially in the past, and all these are to be credited to the strikes without which there would have been no trades-unions.

(Concluded next month.)

IF you want roughly to estimate any one's mental calibre, you cannot do it better than by observing the ratio of generalities to personalities in his talk—how far simple truths about individuals are replaced by truths abstracted from numerous experiences of men and things.—*Spencer's Sociology.*

A LONDON paper, in tracing the mode in which 122 titled families have acquired land, states that not one-tenth of the 5,500,000 acres they possess was acquired by giving value therefor.

THE CONVICT.

CHAPTER V.

Who are the Thenardiers?

We will say one word about them for the present, and complete the sketch hereafter. These beings belong to the bastard class, composed of coarse parvenues, and of degraded people of intellect, which stands between the classes called the middle and lower, and combines some of the faults of the second with nearly all the vices of the first; though without possessing the generous impulse of the working man or the honest regularity of the tradesman.

Theirs were those dwarf natures which easily become monstrous, when any gloomy fire accidentally warms them. There was in the woman the basis of a witch, in the man the stuff for a beggar. Both were in the highest degree susceptible of that sort of hideous progress which is made in the direction of evil.

It is not enough to be bad in order to prosper: and the pot-house was a failure. Thanks to the fifty-seven francs, Thenardier had been able to avoid a protest, and honor his signature; but the next month they wanted money again, and his wife took to Paris and pledged Cosette's outfit for sixty francs. So soon as this sum was spent, the Thenardiers grew accustomed to see in the little girl a child whom they had taken in through charity, and treated her accordingly. As she had no clothes, she was dressed in the left-off chemises and petticoats of the little Thenardiers, that is to say in rags. She was fed on the leavings of every body, a little better than the dog, and a little worse than the cat. Dog and cat were her usual company at dinner: for Cosette ate with them under the table off a wooden trencher like theirs.

The mother who had settled, as we shall see hereafter, at M. sur M., wrote, or to speak more correctly had letters written every month to enquire after her child. The Thenardiers invariably replied that Cosette was getting on famously. When the first six month had passed, the mother sent seven francs for the seventh, and continued to send the money punctually month by month. The year was not ended before Thenardier said, "A fine thing that! and what does she expect us to do with seven francs!" and he wrote to demand twelve. And the mother whom they persuaded that her child was happy and healthy, submitted and sent the twelve francs.

If the mother had returned to Montfermeil at the end of three years; she would not have recognized her child. Cosette so pretty and ruddy on her arrival in this house, was now thin and sickly. She had a timid look about her; "It's cunning!" said the Thenardiers. Injustice had made her sulky, and wretchedness had made her ugly. Nothing was left her but her fine eyes which were painful to look at, because they were so large, it seemed as if a greater amount of sadness was visible in them. It was a heart-rending sight to see this poor child, scarce six years old, shivering in winter under her calico rags, and sweeping the street before daybreak, with an enomous broom in her small red hands and a tear in her large eyes.

The country people called her "the lark." The lower classes, who are fond of metaphors, had given the name to the poor little creature, who was no larger than a bird, trembling, frightened, and starting, who was always the first awake in the house and the village, and ever in the street or the fields by daybreak.

There was this difference, however —this poor lark did not sing.

* * * * *

What had become of the mother? where was she? what was she doing? After leaving her little Cosette with the Thenardier, she had continued her journey and arrived at M. sur M. Fantine had been away from her province for ten years, and while she had been descending from misery to misery, her native town had prospered. About two years before, one of those industrial facts which are the events of small towns had taken place. The details are important, and we think it useful to develop them, we might almost say, to understand them.

From time immemorial M. sur M. had as a special trade the imitation of English jet and German black beads. This trade had hitherto only vegatated, owing to the dearness of the material, which reacted on the artisan. At the moment which Fantine returned to M. sur M. an extraordinary transformation had taken place in the production of "black articles." Towards the close of 1815, a man, a stranger, had settled in the town, and had the idea of substituting in this trade gum lac for rosin, and in bracelets particularly, scraps of bent plate for welded plate. This slight change was a revolution, it prodigiously reduced the cost of the material, which, in the first place, allowed the wages to be raised, a benifit for the town; secondly, improved the manufacture, an advantage for the consumer; and thirdly, allowed the goods to be sold cheap, while producing them at a profit, an advantage for the manufacturer.

In less than three years the inventor of the process had become rich, which is a good thing, and had made all rich about him, which is better. He was a stranger in the department; no one knew anything about his origin, and but little about his start. It was said that he had entered the town with but little money, a few hundred francs at the most; but with this small capital, placed at the service of an ingenious idea, and fertilized by regularity and thought, he made his own fortune and that of the town. On his arrival at M. sur M. he had the dress, manners, and language of a working man. It appears that on the very December night when he obscurely entered M. sur M. with his knapsack on his back, and a knotted stick in his hand, a great fire broke out in the Town Hall. This man rushed into the midst of flames, and at the risk of his own life saved two children who happened to belong to the captain of the gendarms; hence no one dreamed of asking for his passport. On this occasion his name was learned; he called himself Father Madeleine. He was a man of about fifty, with a preoccupied air, and he was good-hearted. That was all that could be said of him.

Thanks to the rapid progress of this trade which he had so admirably remodeled, M. sur M. had become a place of considerable trade. Spain, which consumes an immense amount of jet, gave large orders for it annually, and in this trade M. sur M. almost rivalled London and Berlin. Father Madeleine's profits were so great that after the second year he was able to build a large factory, in which were two spacious workshops, one for men, the other for women. Any one who was hungry need only to come, and was sure to find employment and bread.

At the biginning, kind souls said: "He is a man who wants to grow rich;" when it was seen that he enriched the town before he enriched himself, the same charitable souls said, "He is ambitious." This seemed the more likely because he was religious, and even practised to a certain extent a line which was admired in those days.

In 1819, the report spread through the town that, on the recommendation of the Perfect, Father Madeleine was about to be nominated by the

King, Mayor of M. Those who had declared the new-comer an ambitious man, eagerly seized this opportunity to exclaim: "Did we not say so?" All M. was in an uproar; for the rumor was well founded. A few days after, the appointment appeared in the *Moniteur*, and the next day Father Madeleine declined the honor. In the same year the new processes worked by him were shown at the Industrial Exhibition; and on the report of the jury, the King made the inventor a Chevalier of the Legion of Honor. There was a fresh commotion in the little town; "Well it was a cross he wanted," but Father Madeleine declined the cross. Decidedly the man was an enigma, but charitable souls got out of the difficulty by saying, "After all, he is a sort of adventurer."

When he was known to be rich, " people in society " bowed to him, and he was called in the town Monsieur Madeleine, but his workmen and the children continued to call him Father Madeleine, and this caused him to smile. A thousand advances were made to him, but he refused. This time again charitable souls were not thrown out, " He is an ignorant man of poor education. No one knows were he comes from. He could not pass muster in society, and it is doubtful whether he can read." When he was seen to be earning money, they said, "He is a tradesman;" when he scatered his money, they said, "He is ambitious;" when he rejected honor, they said, "He is an adventurer;" and when he repulsed society, they said "He is a brute."

In 1820, five years after his arrival at M. the service he had rendered the town were so brilliant, the will of the whole country was so unanimous, that the king again nominated him Mayor of the Town. He refused again, but the Perfect would not accept his refusal; all the notables came to beg, the people suplicated him in the open streets, and the pressure was so great, that he eventually assented. It was noticed what appeared specially to determine him was the almost angry remark of an old woman, who cried to him from her door: "A good Mayor is useful; a man should not recoil before the good he may be able to do."

Father Madeleine remained as simple as he had been on the first day; he had grey hair, a serious eye, the bronze face of a workman, and the thoughtful face of a philosopher. He performed his duties as mayor, but beyond that lived solitary; he spoke to few persons, liked to escape from compliments, smiled to save himself from laughing, and gave to save himself from smiling. He was affable and sad: people said, "There is a rich man who is not proud, a lucky man who does not look happy." Some persons asserted that he was a mysterious character, and declared that no one ever entered his bed-room, which was a real anchorite's cell. This was so often repeated that some elegant and spiteful liadies of M. came to him one day and said, " Monsieur le Maire, *do* show us your bed-room, for people say it is a grotto." He smiled, and led them straightway to the "grotto;" they were terribly punished for their curiosity, as it was a bed-room, merely containing mahogany furniture as ugly as all furniture of that sort, and hung with a paper at sixpence the piece. They could not see anything but 2 double-branched candlesticks of an antiquated pattern, standing on the mantlepiece, and seemed to be silver. People whispered that he had immense sums with Lafitte, and with this peculiarity that things were at his disposal, "so that," they added, "M. Madeleine could go any morning to Lafitte's, sign a receipt, and carry off his two or three millions of fancs in ten minutes." In reality, these " two or three millions" were reduced, to six hundred and thirty or forty thousand francs.

The Political Situation in California.

From our esteemed correspondent, "Vanguard," of San Francisco, we have received an interesting letter, the essence of which we have summarized for the benefit of our readers. Our correspondent says:

The long expected crisis in the Workingmen's Party of California has now arrived. *Now* is seen the necessity of the "backbone" which keeps up the entire labor movement throughout the world. Now is the time when the radical Socialistic element must assert itself.

Mr. Kearney has proved himself a good organizer. The Workingmen's Party, under his leadership, has done much to wake up the people to some vital issues of a local character. But in the agitation of such leading questions as land, finance, representation, railroads, etc., that party has done but little systematic work. Mr. Kearney is an apologizer for the millionaire stock-gambling "bonanza" firm of Flood & Co., and has in general been very tender in dealing with railroads. It is doubtful if he or any other now prominent man in that party really understand much about vital labor issues. They are not thorough even in the Chinese question, which is their pivotal issue.

Kalloch, elected Mayor by this party, is a political speculator, who probably never did a square day's work in his life; but he can get up a fair speech, and has much personal magnetism.

Freud. the defeated W. P. C. can-

fore stated, is pivoted on the Chinese question; yet the democratic candidate for the presidency is more likely than not to be in favor of Chinese immigration without limit.

Moreover, a land limitation law which nearly passed the State Senate, was rejected on a second reading, four Senators of the Workingmen's Party recording themselves in favor of continued and unrestricted monopoly of the soil.

In my opinion the Workingmen's Party of California has been more of a hindrance than help, in this city, to the formation of a political party on live issues; and radical agitation on labor questions goes on with little or no reference to its operations. The Socialists are not as yet of any strength as a political party; but they are reaching the workingmen generally, their audiences being limited only by the capacity of their hall.

The significance of the charter vote here in March, has been misunderstood on the spot, and will probably be more so in the East. The "Citizen's" ticket represented a union of Republicans and Democrats, and polled 18,854 votes against 11,-447 for the Workingmen's Party. This leaves 15,000 who, by staying away from the polls, said, "A plague on both your houses." Of the 20,-000 who voted with the Workingmen's Party in September last, many were doubtless disgusted at late movements indicating a sell-out to the Democrats.

LABOR is the only universal as well as the only accurate measure of value

Dennis Kearney.

This disturber of the peace, this blatherskite, this slander slinger, this fellow who denounces speculators and stock gamblers for pursuing *their* trades, is at last stowed safely away in the San Francisco penitentiary. Let this be a lesson (as it is intended to be) to those demagogues who find fault with the present disorder of things. Low wages are all right; bossism is all right; flooding the country with cheap Chinese labor is all right. But to complain, or to even hint that there are more equitable ways of carrying on business than our present no-system style— it is this that is wrong, and this is the real crime for which Dennis Kearney is to day in prison.

To show the temerity, the utter recklessness of this man Kearney, we give below the incendiary portion of his speech, and which the most righteous judge used as a pretext for sentencing him to the penitentiary for six months, and also to pay a fine of $1,000:

"They ask for peace. Who is at war? Who is making this turmoil? I never saw the city more peaceful. There's Claus Speckles, the biggest thief who ever went unhung, and I am man enough to tell him so to his face. He induced his men to take an oath to club me, but they dare not do it. I tell you right here. if I hear of any man plotting to kill me, I will kill him. If they kill me, then the insurrection will commence in earnest. They tell me to shut up or leave the city. I propose to stay. I claim this as a right. The only way they can silence me is to kill me. They may lock me up; but to keep me from talking they must cut my tongue out. Even them I want them to remember that the Chinese must go, the thieving stock gamblers must go, and the murdering Council after them. They may do what they please with me, but I want them to count the consequences which come afterward.

Dennis Kearney, it will be seen, has been guilty of a political crime: organizing a Workingmen's Party, and daring to pit it against the combined forces of the capitalistic par-ties. But this much is certain: his imprisonment is a dastardly act—a crowning outrage upon the right of free speech. It illustrates the fact that the machinery of our government is under the control of brutal and corrupt men, who will not scruple to do anything to suppress the agitation now convulsing the world. McDonnell and Menton suffered the prison because they saw a wrong and dared denounce it.

These outrages upon workingmen and their representatives will continue until workingmen rise up en masse in indignation, and say to these lawless vagabonds: "Hold! you will commit these outrages again at your peril." Workingmen, combine to resist these tyrants! Organize! *Educate!!* ACT!!!

A Truly Great Man.

Few men in this heathen society have the moral courage and manliness to do a great humanitarian act without even a hope of reward on earth. Among the few eminently great and consciencious stands Mr. Patrick Ford, editor and proprietor of that beacon of human rights, the *Irish World*. A young man who had been in his employ for five years began stealing letters for his mail a few months ago, and when detected 1,500 letters were found in his possession. How many more were stolen is not known, but the probabilities are that a large number were destroyed. For this betrayal of confidence and trust Mr. Ford refuses to prosecute him, believing that it is neither right nor Christo act revengefully toward a man for what he has done in the past, and that the humiliation he has suffered is punishment enough.

Mr. Ford does not believe our prisons very good reformatory institutions, and regards it as contemptible to deal with severity an ordinary rogue, "while the iniquitous system under which we live licenses a cunning few to steal banks and railroads, to disinherit the millions, to rob labor of the fruits of its industry, and then, through its subsidized press, denounces as infidels those who protest against these anti-christian proceedings, and who would establish justice on earth."

The Religion of the Future.

We give below a few extracts, taken at random, from the pamphlet "God and Man a Unity."

Theology, like science, must become republicanized.

Religion consists in right action towards others and ourselves.

No man or church can set bounds to progress, nor institute usages suitable for all times.

No supernatural heaven has yet been imagined which would satisfy the ordinary human being for a month.

Education, imperfect as it is, has stirred up thought everywhere, while the pressure of poverty incites to rebellious action.

Where one man is dependent on another fo work and bread, he is in social serfdom, and his serf status follows him even into the church.

What every man is, is what his attributes, surroundings and efforts have made him. What he does is what the general tendency of things lead him to do.

Science preaches better sermons than theology. Science leads toward God by teaching codes of physical and moral laws that are indisputable, and which tend to make us more perfect and happy men and women, far in advance of theological imaginings.

No one outside of the wages classes can have an adequate idea of the sufferings and sacrifices of men and women wage-workers in times of low wages and scarcity of employment. It leads to drunkenness, theft, prostitution, and other abuse of humanity. It tends to embrute whole populations, and destroy all moral impulses. What can be expected of classes chained down to the lowest and most debasing conditions of humanity? The home is a dungeon and the workshop a prison, and capital holds the key to both.

Great Molder's Strike.

Friday, May 7th, the Union Molders at the Detroit Stove Works struck on account of the discharge of the Secretary of their Union, but subsequently receded, finding their position untenable, and also that the men would not come out, there being but 50 union men in the shop. They however filed a demand for 25 per cent. advance, which was refused by the Company; and the men went out, and from day to day have captured the remaining hands and got them in their union.

The men work by the piece, and make all the way from 60 cents to $3,50 per day—the general average being about 35 per cent. below the scale of 1873. They not only claim wages are lower than anywhere else, but the work is not equalized—some men can do well, getting all the "fat," and others cannot earn a dollar a day. It is believed the employers will be compelled to yield, as this is the season when fall trade orders are being given out, and a stoppage now will entail emmense loss on the company. The men have some money on hand, are plucky, and feel that the influance of the consolidated Trades Assembly is in their favor.

OUR TRADES Council is growing finely. It now represents eleven unions.

ANY person sending the names of six subscribers and $4.50, will receive on extra copy free.

ONE hundred and twelve circulars returned to the New Jersey Statistical Labor Bureau report nearly 2,000 boys and nearly 1,800 girls employed between the ages of 10 and 15 years, and 101 boys and 60 girls under 10, employed in factories. Thirty-two circulars testify that night work is also performed by the children to a greater or lesser degree.

Kemble & Co.

The bribers of the Pennsylvania legislature have at last been sentenced and—pardoned. They were millionaires, and the penalties of the law are not for such. Prisons are built for the poor. Kemble jumped his bail while awaiting sentence, and paid no attention to the orders of the court. Yet "no officer molested him, and no process was issued for his arrest." But when the promise was given that they should be pardoned before the ink could dry upon their sentences, the bribers condescended to appear at the bar. This is not the way the law treats common criminals. More than this: it prostitutes justice for the sake of silencing the voice of the poor. Behold Dennis Kearney imprisoned for exercising the right of free speech. In this free country, under this people's government (theoretically), it seems practically impossible to get the rich punished when they break the law, even when the crime is committed against the people, "who by the fiction of our system are supposed to govern." Whose fault is it? Reader, are not *you* to blame?

JOHN SINEY is dead. As one of the first organizers of the miners of Pennsylvania, his memory should be revered wherever trades unions exists. Says the *Trades:* " He stood majestically above his fellow men in strenth af intellect and integrity of purpose, as an oak stands above its dwarf surroundings. He was as modest and unassuming as a child

THE LABOR REVIEW.

The Month's Review.

Sixty-seven items in one paper a few days ago reported strikes, compromises and advance in wages. A few unsuccessful strikes were noticed. Such are the indications of a general advance in wages. But are workingmen better off now than a year or two ago? Yes, and no. Those who were idle then, and who are now working, are certainly better circumstanced. But those who have all along held situations are unable to purchase as much with their wages now as they were then, even with an advance of 10 or 15 per cent.

The principal event of interest that has occurred has been the holding of large mass meetings all over the country denouncing the arrest and imprisonment of Dennis Kearney. New York, Boston, Chicago, St. Louis, and scores of other places have issued their whereases and resolves. If these same well-meaning workingmen would only *act* as bravely as they have shouted aye when voting on the resolutions, there would be little likelihood of such another outrage being perpetrated in the United States against the right of free speech. The one held in Boston was addressed by Osborn Ward. He said, among other things, that the Chinese could only be looked on in the light of labor-saving machinery, and with this he touched on one of the objects of Socialism, viz: the placing of all machines directly under the control of the people. The Trades and Labor Coun-

ney as a vile tool of the corruption-
ists and a disgrace to the honorable
possition which he occupies. The
Detroit Council of Trades and Labor Unions passed resolutions of a
similar tone.

The employes of Mr. Kuttnauer,
cigar manufacturer of this city, recently struck against the "poor
stock" given them to work up.

Comrade Parsons writes to the
Paterson *Labor Standard* that the
trades unions of Chicago are quite
active, the signs indicating a concerted move for less hours and more
pay. The railroad freight-house employes who struck for more wages
were unsuccessful, as they were entirely unorganized. The hod carriers and laborers are taking a wiser
course—organizing first.

In New York city $2.50 a day is
now the average wages of journeymen generally, but strikes are
gradually bringing it up to $3—
about $2 too little, considering the
cost of living there.

The circulars issued by the employes of Lorillard & Co., tobacco
manufacturers, New York, have
caused considerable excitement in
this city among tobacco users. Lorillard & Co. require each one of
their employes to sign an agreement
that they and their homes may be
searched *at any time* without warrant of law, to see if any of Lorillard & Co.'s tools or materials have
been stolen. The circular requests
consumers to stop buying Lorillard
& Co.'s brands, and not to trade at
any store that keeps them for sale.
These are their brands: For smoking
and chewing: Tin Tag, Eureka, Century, Cap Sheet A, Kilkenney Cut,
Rose Leaf and Climax Tin Tag. For
smoking only: Yacht Club, Bullion,
Cavendish, Drawing Room Tobacco
and Cigarettes,Snuffs, etc.

From a recent number of the
Australasian and Sketcher we glean
the following facts: The labor market is fully supplied. Domestic ser-

vants receive £35 per annum. Those
employed in the building trades average 10s. per day; laborers 7s. per
day; printers 1s. per 1,000 (but
whether for *ms* or *ns* it does not
state); ship carpenters 13s. for 8
hours; and miners from £2 to £2 5s.
per week. Other trades run from
8s. to 11s. per day.

Some of the cabinet makers in
Grand Rapids, Mich., have succeeded in breaking up the practice of being paid in store orders.——The
press-feeders in several large printing offices in Chicago have had an
increase of a dollar a week in their
wages; but they had first to strike.
——There are at least five miners'
strikes now in progress.——Cigar-
makers generally are demanding an
advance of from 50c. to $1 a thou-
sand.

And so the work goes on, a gradual rise in prices being perceived in
nearly all trades.

Notes by the Way.

C. H. LITCHMAN, the well known
crispin and labor agitator, is expected to deliver one or two lectures in
Detroit the first week in June.

HAVING submitted their difficulties
with their employers to arbitration,
the English iron workers lately on a
strike have resumed work at a 5 per
cent. reduction.

IF manufacturers are allowed to
have a tariff to keep out the cheap
fabrics from foreign countries, why
should not workingmen be allowed
a tariff to keep out the cheap labor
from China?

PRESIDENT A. Owen, D. D., of
Denison University, Ohio, has written a strong article to the *Christian
Hearld*, Detroit, against the third
termers. He closes as follows: "If
it be really true, as Grant's supporters argue, that the country is in such
peril that he is the only man who
can save it, then I say it is lost already, and no man can save it."

THE Cincinnati *Exponent* has been enlarged to an eight-page paper. Don't grow too fast, brother.

' FRENCH papers state there are 250,000 persons awaiting means of transportation to this county.

"THE Lords cause is progressing," writes a correspondent to a Detroit religious weekly; " we are about to shingle our house of worship." Selah.

THERE is to be a convention of promient labor men in Boston, May 26, to consider the best systen for agitation on the Ten Hour Question.

WE HOPE none of our readers will fail to read "Trades Unions and Strikes," on our second page. Comrade Smart makes some points his opponents will do well to think twice over before attempting to refute.

WITHOUT divergence from beaten paths, from that which exists, whether it be in politics or religion, there can be no progress. *Radicalism* is necessary for growth. While temporary ills may accompany the divergence, these are far out-balanced by the eventual good.

A CERTAIN D. D. in this city preached against the sin of dancing, remarking in the course of his wise dissertation that "young men who received $15 or $20 a week" required all their wages for *necessities* of life. We wonder if the reverend gentleman realizes that the workingmen—the producers—of Detroit receive on an average less than $9 a week.

THE PRINTERS of Detroit, Flint and Bay City have called a convention of all the printers in the state to meet in this city on May 21st, for the purpose of organizing a State Aid society,or Mutual BenefitAssociation to provide for members sick and out of work; social intercourse; to establish a typographical intelligence office; and anything else thought necessary.

THE Chicago Packingmen's Protective and Benevolent Union, the organazation which inaugurated the mammoth strike at the stock yards last winter, and which at one time comprised nearly ten thousand members, is reported as vitually disbanded. At a called meeting, recently, only twenty-seven members appeared, and none of them were willing to accept office.

AS CONSUMERS, a rise in the price of products falls more heavily on the vast number who work for wages, than on the small number who have moderate or large incomes. But as producers, a rise of prices, by stimulating trade and giving employment, is, as, a whole, of benefit to wages-workers.

THE RESTRICTION of the number of apprentices, the increase of wages in organized trades at the expense of the unorganized ones, and the cultivation of the sin of selfishness, are unavoidable accompaniments of trades unions. But nevertheless trades unions are needful for self defence. The selfishness of the employer can only be met by selfishnes on the part of the employed. Severe diseases require severe remedies. Every step made by humanity towards a higher plane of civilization brought some temporary evil with it. But the evil finally disappears leaving the good a heritage for future generations. The evils of trades unions are evils involved in the transition to the better arrangements, and they too, will in due time disappear.

A WRITER in the New York *Sun* estimates that for a family to " Go West" and be successful, it would require at least $900. This cry of "Go West" sound well, but how are the poor to get there without help? Silly editors, who draw good salaries and sit in their comfortable offices, think they have settled the labor problem when they write a trashy editorial about the place for surplus labor is on the broad acres of the west, never giving a thought of how the unfortune laborer is to get there. These same shallow-pated fools then scratch off another "editorial" about the absurdity of Wright's Land Bill. And so it goes; and so it will go until the people see that it is to their interest to give those who are willing to go material aid through the goverment. It will not only benefit those who stay, by reducing the competition between them, drawing off the surplus labor.

THE army and Anti-Socialists bills in Germany and the land troubles in England are sending to our shores multidudes of emigrants. In 1814 319,000 reached our shores—the maximum. In 1877 but 55,000 came—the minimum. But this year over 400,-000 are coming. The emigrants are largely skilled workmen, and not a few bring considerable means. Nearly 5,000 left in a single week lately from Breman, Germany.

IN the Voigtland district, Saxony a majority of the people are engaged in the manufacture of lace curtains. The highest earnings paid a skilled workman in this business is 75 cents a week. If every member of the family works, as they must, they can earn 26 cents a day, or $1.73 per week. On the average, five persons must live on this income. And now Secretary Evarts tells us that the workingmen of this country must make up their minds not to be any better off than their brothers in the old world. Well he is right. Under our present industrial system it is but a matter of time when the free born American laborer will be working for 75 cents a week.

WANTED—An Agent in every town in the United States to canvass for THE LABOR REVIEW. See terms to agents. Address all communications to this office.

SOCIALISTIC LABOR PARTY.

FURNISHED BY THE SECRETARY, PHILIP VAN PATTEN.

NATIONAL EXECUTIVE COMMITTEE.

P. C. Christiansen........128 Antoine st.
Charles Erb............ 579 Dequinde st.
Judson Grenell..........116 Howard st.
Gustav Herzig...........29 Napoleon st.
Philip Van Patten.........P. O. Box 597
E. W. Simpson, Rec.Sec'y..90 Wilkins st.
Wm. Kuess............. 556 Clinton ave.

The Chicago Labor Convention.

The National Executive Committee of the Socialistic Labor Party issues the following Special Call:

To all Trade and Labor Organizations, Eight Hour Leagues,Liberal and Radical Reform Associations, etc., contemplating participation by delegates in the Labor Convention in Chicago on June 9th.

FRIENDS AND COMRADES: However varying and conflicting may be the opinions held by our respective organizations with regard to the expediency of most of the measures hitherto proposed as remedies for societary evils, yet upon the question of what is and ought to be the immediate duty of the national government, there is but one opinion, one voice, one unalterable decision! That highest of all laws, the law of Eminent Domain, must be asserted and enforced! The Government must retain its sovereignty and perpetuate our republican institutions by maintaining such control over Land, Labor and Money, the sources of wealth and the instruments of exchange, that equal rights and opportunities shall be secured to all citizens. The recognition by the American people of this fundamental principle will [open the way for the accomplishment of the radical reforms necessary for its practical application.

Desirous of obtaining unity of all progressive elements represented at at Chicago, upon the most essential measures, and knowing the need of proper joint deliberation before engaging in the important work of the final Convention, we hereby invite all delegates who sympathize with the objects of this call, to meet with those of the Socialistic Labor Party, on June 8th, in Chicago, at such place as will be made known through the daily papers, for the purpose of reaching an agreement whereby harmonious action may be assured for the support of such candidates and measures as we can consistently endorse.

PHILIP VAN PATTEN,
Party Sec'y.
Detroit, May 17, 1880.

——o——

Financial Report of the Executive Committee for April.

RECEIPTS.

Balance on hand at last report.....	$2 01
Buffalo section, dues	80
St. Louis do	27 90
Davenport do	65
Lawrence do	5 30
New Haven, M. Tiedemann, pamp'ts	40
Milwaukee Section, dues..........	1 50
New Market, Min., H. Brewer, pam'ts	24
Indianapolis Section, dues	8 20
Baltimore, A. Reinle, constitutien	10
Utica, N. Y., Section, dues	8 95
Milwaukee do	1 45
Paul Reinherd, (single member) ...	1 00
A. D. Wheeler, pamphlets	1 00
Pittsburgh Section, dues..........	5 50
Courtney, Pa., three members... ..	1 50
Buffalo, N. Y., Vander Willegin ..	13
Chicago Section, on account.......	100 00
Manchester Section, dues	7 00
	$168 68

EXPENDITURES.

Rent of P. O. Box	$2 50
Printing................	1 50
Current expenses, postage, etc....	7 52
Salary of Secretary, five weeks	60 00
	$71 52

Balance, cash on hand, $92.11.

——o——

Comrade Osborn Ward spoke in Lawrence, Mass., on May 1st, and at last accounts was making a tour through the New England States.

Party News.

Our new Section in Buffalo is flourishing, and so is the new weekly started by Comrade Erhart.

The Irish World continues to spread the truth in its liberal and fearless manner. Who says that Socialism is not making progress?

A new Section in Cincinnati is waiting to be adopted as soon as the Party vote upon the expulsion of the former one shall have been completed.

The "California Free Press," published at San Francisco, is a German weekly which now boldly champions the cause of Socialism. Welcome to the ranks!

The author of "The Coming Revolution," Comrade Groenlund, is now in Boston, where he is delivering a course of lectures on Socialism before cultivated audiences.

Our membership at New Orleans has united with the trades unions of that city in publishing a lively English weekly paper, called the "Workingmen's Union Advocate."

BOB. INGERSOLL and the Liberal Leaguers have not yet fully recovered from the electric shock recieved last September at Cincinnati. Come friends, what are you going to do?

The proposed paper in the English language in New York city has failed to materialize, as the risk is almost too great for our membership at present. Slow and sure, is now our motto.

Comrade Franz, of Chicago, will soon go to Cincinnati to assume the editorial management of the new German workingmen's paper there, according to information furnished the Executive.

The Spring election at Chicago resulted in the polling of about 6,000 votes for the Socialistic ticket, and the election of several aldermen. Two of them are swindled out of their victory, however, by ballot-

Co-operation has been described as "the concert of many for com- passing advantages impossible to be reached by one, in order that the gain made may be fairly shared by all concerned in its attainment." It has not been possible, so far in the history of co-operation, to arrive at a result the profit of which may be confined alone to those engaged in the work done.

Generally others have contributed capital to a greater or less extent, and frequently the interest of the capitalists concerned has dominated over that of the laborers, resulting finally in ordinary business enter- prises divested of co-operative fea- tures.

Co-operation received a great im- pulse in France at the time of the French revolution of 1848. That revolution was a republican and es- sentially a workingmen's movement, and following upon its heels were laws passed favorable to, and money appropriated for, co-operative so- cieties. These societies were not based upon any thoroughly digest- ed plan, in fact rather upon theories demonstrated by doctrainaires than upon forms justified by experience. This was, in the nature of things, unavoidable. When, however, Na- poleon the Third found himself seat- ed securely upon his throne, he per- mitted co-operative societies to per- ish, and frowned upon all working- men's movements.

When the first steps were taken toward this co-operative experiment referred to, several French states- men expressed themselves as to the success it would probably meet with. The words of M. Thiers are worthy of notice.

Said he: "The invention of work- ingmen's associations is worthy of companionship with the others we have seen spring into existence with- in a few years, and beyond all no- tions of good sense and impractical. The first question which presents

itself is to know from what source one can draw the capital of these as- sociations. Capital can only be furnished by a capitalist or by stock- holders. But, let us ask, who will ever furnish capital to a collective association, to a workingmen's as- sociation? Assuredly, no one. There is but one capitalist to fur- nish associations of this kind; there is but one to which any one could advise such a great folly:—that is the State. A collection of workmen can be neither vigilant, nor strict, nor strong in will, nor economical, nor enlightened, as it is necessary they should be in order to direct with success an industrial enterprise. A master who cannot discharge his workmen, grade their salaries ac- cording to their merit, oblige them to work with such or such activity, or himself resolve, and that imme- diately, cannot prosper. Working- men's associations are nothing more than anarchy in industry."

M. Clement said: "We are pro- foundly convinced that all research- es tending to establish this new sys- tem of voluntary associations for the purposes of ameliorating the lot of the workmen, are absolutely vain; and that, in order to be efficacious, the efforts of those who interest themselves in the cause of the work- ingmen should be directed in other channels."

Many French statesmen differed from those already cited. Louis Blanc believed in a certain sort of voluntary association. Louis Rey- band believed that the future be- longed to associations. Joseph Gar- nier, while he did not believe that associations could be so generally adopted as to give a new form to industry, and do away with the pro- letariat, thought that nevertheless certain workingmen under certain conditions could unite their efforts and form associations for labor, from which they could withdraw beyond their salary a part of the profits.

The French societies also found strenuous defenders in John Stuart Mill and other English political economists.

In America the question of co-operation has not been discussed to the same extent as in England or France. The reason is that the condition of the wage worker here has been much better, the pressure for means of existence not so great. We have been able to note, however, the increasing difficulty with which workingmen find avenues for employment in the large cities of the East, and the crowded condition of many trades. During our recent panic a partial relief was found in the emigration to, and development of, our western territories. The time is fast coming, however, when this will afford little relief, and a better state of affairs may only be secured in a different apportionment of the profits of labor. This, it is believed, can be attained largely through the establishment of co-operative societies; for then profits would be fairly divided among those engaged in the work.

Granted that co-operation is beneficial, which I think needs no discussion among workingmen, the question for consideration is: How can co-operative associations best be established?

We should commence by the establishment of Trades Assemblies. When these are founded and are thorough in their organization, we have a platform upon which to work. We have a large body of men in

trades should be put upon a co-operative basis.

At the commencement, it is necessary to avoid failure. It is truly argued that a single failure in its shock to the confidence of workingmen, does more harm than can be remedied by half a dozen successes.

What will be the safest manner in which to begin? We have to contend against that want of capital which Thiers pronounces one of the chief difficulties in the way of workingmen's associations. We desire to proceed gradually and safely, and with that design commence with the branch of industry which requires the smallest investment of capital in the beginning, such as painting, carpentering, masonwork or tailoring.

The stock necessary to be subscribed could be taken exclusively by those connected with the Assembly, or under its jurisdiction, the attempt being made to limit it to workingmen alone, or preferably to those of the trade involved. Owing to the small amount of capital required to place the first trades association upon its feet, commencements in others could speedily be made.

Branches requiring the investment of considerable sums could be gradually interested, profiting meanwhile by the experience of their predecessors. Money might be paid in by easy and lengthened instalments and in a few years the town might possess a score of active, flourishing co-operative enterprises.

The design could be borne in mind

certain number—say a million or two millions, it matters not how many—

THEY WOULD STRIKE

once and forever, never to take up tool again, except their *own* tools; on their *own* materials, in their *own* factories or workshops, or in their *own* mines, or on their *own* land, and to have the product of their labor for their *own* property;—*then*, I should have faith in trades unions.

But I have no such expectation. *I see in trades unions no tendency in that direction.*

In the broad sense in which I am now considering the subject of trades unions, I consider them injurious to the best interests of the laboring classes, because, even for the narrow purposes they have in view, they have outlived their usefulness —their adequacy. They are as powerless to resist concentrated capital as wooden war-ships are to resist the concentrated power of modern artillery.

But the worst fault they have is that they obstruct radical and practicable labor movements.

They keep up ancient superstitions of political economy. They are among the chief props of the present iniquitous and absurd industrial system. They stand in the way of the education of the laboring classes in a true knowledge of their condition and of the only means to improve. They are among the worst "rocks ahead" of Socialism. They mislead Socialists themselves into a support and endorsement of them, false and insincere in proportion to the intelligence of such political and compromising Socialists. They are the cause why the platforms of Socialists are weakened with inconsistencies. They cause the banner of Socialism to be disfigured by absurdities. They are the means of introducing persons who are not Socialists into our ranks, and thus influencing Socialists to support unsocialistic measures and movements. They so bring merited ridicule and contempt upon our cause.

For all these reasons and many more, trades unions, in their general influence upon the labor movement, are both negatively and positively injurious to the laboring classes.

"The Light of Asia."

The teachings of, and traditions concerning Buddha, the greatest God of all the gods of the millions of Asia, has been worked into a superb and entrancing poem by Dr. Arnold. Below is a short extract that might be appropriately headed:

EACH MAN HIS PRISON MAKES.

Pray not! the Darkness will not brighten!
Ask naught from Silence, for it cannot
  speak!
Vex not your mournful minds with pious
  pains!
Ah! Brothers, Sisters! seek
Naught from the helpless gods by gift and
  hymn,
Nor bribe with blood, nor feed with fruit
  and cakes;
Within yourself deliverance must be sought;
  Each man his prison makes.
Each hath such lordships as the loftiest ones;
  Nay, for with Powers above, around, below,
As with all flesh, and whatsoever lives,
  Act maketh joy or woe,
What hath been, bringeth what shall be,
  and is
  Worse—better—last for first, and first for
  last;
The Angels in the Heaven of Gladness reap
  Fruits of a holy past.
The devils in the underworld wear out
  Deeds that were wicked in an age gone by.
Nothing endures! fair virtues waste with
  time,
  Foul sins grow purged thereby,
Who toiled a slave may come anew a Prince,
  For gentle worthiness and merit won;
Who ruled a King may wander earth in rags,
  For things done and undone.
Higher than Indra's ye may lift your lot;
  And sink it lower than the worm or gnat,
The end of many myriad lives is this,
  The end of myriads that.
Only, while turns this wheel invisible,
  No pause, no peace, no staying-place can
  be;
Who mounts will fall, who falls may mount;
  the spokes
Go round unceasingly.

THE CONVICT.

CHAPTER VI.

At the beginning of 1821, the papers announced the decease of M. Myriel, Bishop of D——, and who died in the odour of sanctity at the age of eighty-two. The announcement was copied by the local papers of M——, and on the next day Monsieur Madeleine appeared dressed in black, with crape on his hat.

By degrees and with time all the opposition to Father Madeleine died out. Only one man in the town resisted, and whatever M. Madeleine might do, remained rebellious to it, as if a sort of incorruptible and imperturbable instinct kept him on his guard. This person, who was grave, with an almost menacing gravity, was one of those men who, though only noticed for a moment, preoccupy the observer. His name was Javert, and he belonged to the police, and preformed duties of an inspector. He had not seen Madeleine's beginning. When Javert arrived at M——, the great manufacturer's fortune was made, and Father Madeleine had become Monsieur Madeleine.

The Austrian peasants are convinced that in every litter of wolves there is a dog which is killed by the mother, for, otherwise, when it grew it would devour the other whelps. Give a human face to this dog-son of a she-wolf, and we shall have Javert. He was born in prison; his mother was a fortune-teller, whose husband was at the galleys.

Javert was like an eye ever fixed on M. Madeleine, an eye full of suspicion and conjectures. He appeared to know, and sometimes said covertly, that some one had obtained certain imformation in a certain district about a certain family which had disappeared. Once he happened to say, speaking to himself. "I believe that I have got him;" then he remained thoughtful for three days without saying a word. It seems that the thread which he fancied he held was broken.

Such was the state of the town when Fantine returned to it. No one remembered her, but luckily the door of M.; Madeleine's factory was like a friendly face; she presented herself at it, and was admitted to the female shop. As the trade was quite new to Fantine, she was awkward at it and earned but small wages; but that was enough, for she had solved the problem—she was earning her livelihood. When Fantine saw that she could live by it, she had a moment of joy. To live honestly by her own toil, what a favor of Heaven! A taste for work really came back to her; she bought a looking glass, delighted in seeing in it her youth, her fine hair and fine teeth; forgot many things, only thought of Cosette, and her possible future, and was almost happy. She hired a small room and furnished it, on credit, to be paid for out of her future earnings—this was a relic of her irregular habits.

Not being able to say that she was married, she was very careful not to drop a word about her child. At the outset, as we have seen, she punctually paid the Thenardiers, and as she could only sign her name, she was compelled to write to them through the agency of a public writer. It was noticed that she wrote frequently. It was begining to be whispered in the shop that Fantine "wrote letters" and was "carrying on."

Fantine was observed then, and besides, more than one girl was jealous of her light hair and white teeth. It was noticed that she often wiped away a tear in the shop; it was when she was thinking of her child, perhaps of the man she had loved. It is painful labor to break off all the gloomy connecting links with the past. It was a fact that she wrote, almost twice a month, and always the same address: "Monsieur Then-ardier, Publican, Montfermeil." The public writer, who could not fill his stomach with wine, without emptying his pockets of secrets, was made to talk at the wine-shop; and, in short, it was known that Fantine had a child. A gossip undertook to journey to Montfermeil, spoke to the Thenardiers, and on her return said, "I do not begrudge my five-and-thirty francs, for I have seen the child."

All this took time, and Fantine had been more than a year at the factory, when one morning the forewoman handed her 50 francs in the Mayor's name, and told her that she was no longer engaged, and had better leave the town, so the Mayor said. It was in this very month that the Thenardiers, after asking for 12 francs instead of 7, raised a claim of 15 instead of 12. Fantine was startled; she could not leave the town, for she owed her rent and for her furniture, and 50 francs would not pay those debts. She stammered a few words of entreaty, but the forewoman intimated to her that she must leave the shop at once: moreover, Fantine was but an indifferent workwoman. Crushed by shame more than disgrace, she left the factory, and returned to her room; her fault then was now known to all. She did not feel the strength to say a word; she was advised to see the Mayor, but did not dare do so. The Mayor gave her 50 francs because he was kind, and discharged her because he was just; and she bowed her head to the sentence.

M. Madeleine, however, knew nothing of all this; and they were combinations of events of which the world is full. M. Madeleine made it a rule hardly ever to enter the female workroom; he had placed at its head an old maid, whom the cure had given him, and he had entire confidence in her. She was really a respectable, firm, equitable and just person, full of that charity which consists in giving, but not possesing to the same extent the charity which comprhends and pardons. M. Madeleine trusted to her in everything, for the best men often delegate their authority, and it was with this full power, and in the conviction that she was acting rightly, that the forewoman tried, condemned, and executed Fantine. As for the 50 francs, she had given them out of a sum M. Madeliene had given her for alms and helping the workwomen, and which she did not account for.

Fantine tried to get a servant's place in the town, and went from house to house, but no one would have anything to do with her.

She could not leave the town, for the broker to whom she was in debt for the furniture—what furniture!—said to her: "If you go away I will have you arrested as a thief." The landlord to whom she owed the rent said to her: "You are young and pretty, you can pay." She divided the 50 francs between the landlord and the broker, gave back to the latter three-fourths of the goods, only retaining what was absolutely necessary, and found herself without work, without a trade, with only a bed, and still owing about 100 francs. She set to work making coarse shirts for the troops, and earned at this sixpence a day, her daughter costing her fourpence.

It was at this moment she began to fall in arrears to the Thenardiers. An old woman, however, taught her the way to live in wretchedness. Behind living on little there is living on nothing—the first is obscure, the second quite dark.

Fantine learned how she could do entirely without fire in winter; how she must get rid of a bird that cost her a half-penny every two days; how she could make a petticoat of her blanket and a blanket of her petticoat, and how candle can be saved by taking your meals by the light of the window opposite. We do not know all that certain weak beings, who have grown old in want and honesty, can get out of a half penny, and in the end it becomes a talent. Fantine acquired this sublime talent, and regained a little courage. At this period she said to a neighbor, "Nonsense, I say to myself; by only sleeping for five hours and working all the others at my needle, I shall always manage to earn bread at any rate. And then, when you are sad, you eat less. Well! suffering, anxiety, a little bread on one side and sorrow on the other, all will support me."

In this distress it would have been a strange happiness to have her daughter with her. But she owed the Thenardiers, and besides had no money to pay traveling expenses.

(To be continued.)

The Plunderers and the Plundered.

A correspondent writes us as follows: I cannot say that I feel so sanguine of an immediate realization of liberty to wage workers. The greatest fraud now in full force and vigor is our educational fraud. Capital, protected by its lying shibboleth fortified by precedent, by tradition, and entrenched behind the sacred teachings of the altar and the pulpit, is destined to make a vigorous fight, and yet lead the masses to a greater submission to its rule. But this will precipitate the long delayed revolution. The swift enforcement of its own iron rule will be the medium of its own destruction. Go on with your glowing, burning, glorifying work of discontent. If there be any moral purpose we should pursue, it is to irritate men against their status. We are the sworn enemies of tranquil forbearance, and our heart's desire is to league in massed opposition against the grinding, perfidious, bastard legalizing of spoil,

stomach, back, life, love and all the elements and attributes which we group within the word *soul.* We talk of mankind being selfish. This is an error. If they are, their selfishness is of a very effiminate description, and to little purpose. What selfishness is there in the millions allowing the few hundreds to chalk off earth's acres, including all its coal and iron, and other natural provisions of fabulous value and infinite need, and submitting to the humiliation of paying in the labor of their lives for the privilege of the use of their own labor and the productions of nature? Is not this splendid scoundrelism? Eminent artistic villainy? Sometimes — not often — these brilliant and cultivated brigands or simpering fools will condescend to sympathise with us; or possibly make themselves agreeable at election time, and the cur-like workingman is the first to apologize for the wrong done by saying, "Well, So-and-so is not such a bad fellow, after all." But this does not lessen the robbery. Nevertheless, these men are no worse than society makes them. They are merely its products. To make their plundering legitimate and profitable there must of course be a sufficient number of people in society who are willing to be legitimately plundered. What we most need is a new moral code. Justice cannot even be approximated under present societary conditions. What is right and just can only be discovered by the application of natural laws. Deluded by fraudulent theories, we have lost sight of justice in the gloom of custom. Disinterestedness, not selfishness, has been the greatest barrier to human progress and freedom.

A SWISS COLONY numbering 700 has settled in Tennessee, and devotes its energies entirely to cheese

The Ownership of Land.

At the Chicago Greenback Labor Convention the Socialists made their fight over the following resolution:

We declare that land, light, air and water are made the free gifts of nature to all mankind. Any law or custom of society that allows any person to monopolize more of these natural' gifts than he has a right to, to the detriment of the rights of others, we earnestly condemn, and seek to abolish.

The greatest question of this age is the question of the right of individuals to own land. It is being put to nearly every nation on the globe, demanding a clear and well defined answer. Interrogators want to know by what right the individual claims thousands of acres of land and charges the tillers of it rent. The people of Ireland feel the great injustice inflicted upon mankind by this iniquitous system, and although the remedy proposed by them will not cure the evil, they have done a great good by bringing this basic wrong before the world and directing thought toward it. They have put that thing called private landed property upon trial, and the nations of the earth are anxiously awaiting the verdict.

Is it consistent with justice that land be private property? Is it not equally consistent with justtice that air and water also be private property? All are gifts of nature, and the right of ownership should be equally good in all. Nations and individuals have even laid claim to water privileges, but these claims have been few, and based upon improvements made. The claims based upon improvements were just, but upon natural water advantages no claim is valid. That individual would be declared insane who would "conquer" thousands of square miles of the ocean and lay claim to it as private property. But would not the claim of the *water*-lord be as consistent as is that of the *land*-lord?

No more right exists in land as private property than in water. If we admit the right of private ownership in land, we must admit the right of the individual to own as much of it as he can buy. No one has the right to trespass on the property of another. Now, let us suppose that a man like Vanderbilt concludes to buy land with merely his income, which is some $3,500 a day. Putting the average price of land at $25 an acre, he would be able to buy 51,100 acres a year, and in 100 years the present income on his fortune would buy 5,110,000 acres of land—more than 7,984 square miles—over which one person could have control, by the present possessor dying and leaving one heir. At the same rate, in 100 years, 451 such fortunes would be able to buy the whole United States. Of course such a thing is not probable, but it comes within the possibilities. The system that even admits of such a possibility is wrong, and a monstrous perversion of true economy. It is repugnant to every idea of democracy, and revolting to the principle of a government for the people. The tendency under such a system is inevitably toward the monopolization of land,—the means of life,—by the few, which is the cause of poverty and the curse of nations.

Everybody should give this land question earnest thought. If they do, they will soon see the injustice of making the means of life of the people property over which a few individuals have full control. Suppose the landlords of Great Britain should conclude not to allow their lands to be tilled at all for a year or two, what would the consequence be? "Ah!" you say, "but the government would not allow such a thing." Then why does not the government take the enormous power away from the landlords and control the land itself? If it has the right to compel the tillage of land, it has the right to control it altogether. The remedy to this giant wrong admits of no half-way measure. It must be absolute. It must be just.

The Printers' International Convention,

The International Typographical Union met in Chicago June 7 and closed its session on the 11th. The dispute between the two factions in St. Louis regarding a charter was amicably settled, and it is hoped hereafter they will work harmoniously together. Printers, as well as other craftsmen, must recognize the fact that only by the unification of the men in their own trade, as well as by the uniting of the different trades societies, will they ever be able to retain from the employing class a larger share of the products of their labor. Subordinate unions were given discretionary powers to receive German Typographical Union cards or not. Sympathy was extended to the printers of Milan, Italy, and money contributed to their relief ordered sent to Mr. J. H. Ralston, Quincy, Ill.

An alleged organization called the Brotherhood of the Union, was resolved unlawful, and the members thereof upon conviction are to be deprived of the right of membership in subordinate unions.

Mayor Prince, of Boston, was censured for establishing a printing office on Deer Island, and doing the work with convicts, and the printers actually resolved to use all honorable means in their power to defeat him and his candidates for further political honors. There is your only remedy, gentlemen. The ballot box is your only hope, disguise it as you will.

A new plan of organization was enacted.

The receipts of the year was $3,-056.30, and expenditures $1,634.80. Salaries were fixed as follows: President, $250; secretary and treasurer, $450; corresponding secretary, $150; sergt.-at-arms, $35; messenger, $25. Mr. Rastall's system of measurement was unanimously adopted.

The subject of uniting trades unions more closely was discussed at length, and the secretary was instructed to issue invitations to all international and national trades unions and trades assemblies in the United States and British provinces to send properly accredited delegates to a convention, to be called hereafter, for the purpose of organizing a continental federation of trades, to meet annually.

The next place of meeting is Toronto.

The Molders' Strike.

We record with gratification the termination of this strike in favor of the men. The *Truthteller* of June 19 says:

The iron molders' strike has ended. On Saturday the Stove Works sent for a committee of the strikers, and after a long conference covering the entire dispute, the men were asked back on a five per cent. increase. A meeting of the molders decided to accept the terms, and on Monday morning the whole gang marched in a body to the shop and began work.

This strike lasted five weeks and has been the longest and most important one ever occurring in Detroit. The men think they have won a practical victory, as they not only obtain a material advance but secure their "discounts" weekly—that is, a statement of the imperfect work for which reductions are made. They have hitherto been unable to obtain this, and consequently have never been sure of what they were to receive on pay-day.

The strikers have held together well, having lost only 25 or 30, chiefly by shipping to other points. Owing to the generous contributions of the other trades and the $75 accruing from the picnic, they have got through without suffering, and consider that they have done well. They might have stood out longer, but the shop was being filled with importations, and there began to be danger that they would lose it entirely.

The account then stands : Five weeks lost ; five per cent. gained, the Union raised from 50 to 150 members, and the shop made practically a union shop.

The men deserve great praise for the quiet manner in which they have conducted themselves during the contest. There was no violence or any suggestion of any, no drunkenness, very little tippling, but only a calm and patient waiting for the result. There was nothing whatever of the bluster and arrogance which have disgraced the labor cause elsewhere.

----o----

Convention Echoes.

Noisy and sassy? Oh, no.

We wonder if the "gentleman" from Tennessee" has that frog still in his throat, ∖

"Points of Order" and "Questions of Privilege," were thicker than whortleberries in fly-time.

Two-thirds of the Convention was thoroughly imbued with Socialistic ideas, and had it not been for a few political trimmers who were afraid to speak the truth above a whisper for fear of losing some middleman's vote, a platform would have been adopted sound to the core.

Persistent Delegate— Mr. Speaker, I offer an amend—"

Speaker—Amendments are out of order.

Del.—Then I offer as a substi—"

Speaker—Substitutes are out of order.

Del.—Then I rise to a question of privi—

Speaker—No question of privilege can be allowed.

Del.—Then I rise to a point of order.

Speaker—State your point of order.

(Persistent delegate then proceeds to offer his amendment under his "point of order," until choked off by the howls of the convention.)

The way Dennis Kearney was sat upon by the women was beautiful to contemplate. Dennis made the statement that if he should favor female suffrage his wife would greet him with a flat-iron instead of a kiss. Then one of the ladies replied in substance as follows: "I am glad to know who is boss in Dennis Kearney's house."

----o----

Notes by the Way.

OUR present social system is a mockery of justice and equity.

- - - -

THE trunkmakers of Boston have established a co-operative shop, which is proving highly successful. They have large orders on hand at good paying prices.

- - - -

A. A. AVERY of Peoria, Ill., is starting a new labor paper there. Give him all the support you can. Workingmen, support the men who advocate your cause.

- - - -

The world must be made too hot for the rascals who now control it. We must continue to preach radicalism and damn conservatism, until just sentiments pervade society.

CAPITAL is determined to reign supreme over Labor; and knowing that human nature will break out in violence when at the "last ditch," it is quietly digging that ditch and commanding it with guns. But what if Labor should organize and consolidate? Are workingmen blind not to see that salvation must come only through organization?—*J. F. Bray.*

"EMPLOYERS." It is a noble title. If, indeed, they have found you idle, and given you employment, wisely, let us no more call them mere "Men" of Business, but rather "Angels" of Business; quite the best sort of Guardian Angel. Yet are you sure it is necessary, absolutely, to look to superior natures for employment? Is it inconceivable that you should employ—yourselves?—*John Ruskin.*

AN agitation meeting on Sunday, June 19, in Arbeiter Hall, by the Socialistic Labor Party, was well attended. The delegates to the Chicago Convention made their report, and speeches were delivered by Messrs. Simpson, Herzig, Van Patten, Labadie and Blair. The radical utterances of the speakers were enthusiastically applauded.

THE cigarmakers of Baltimore, after a ten weeks' strike, have succeeded in getting the prices they demanded. In Utica they are still out, and firm. In Chas. Goss' shop, Philadelphia, the men struck against the foreman. The lockout in St. Paul, ended June 11, the employers concluding to employ Union men.

JUST as Garrison advocated the *immediate abolition of slavery*, so we advocate the *immediate* abolition of private capital and private enterprise. First, because it is morally wrong. Secondly, because it is economically and politically wrong; and third, because its immediate abolition is indispensable to the "life, liberty and happiness" of the people.— *W. G. H. Smart.*

SOCIETY is fully entitled to abrogate or alter any particular right of property which on sufficient consideration it judges to stand in the way of public good. And assuredly the terrible case which Socialists are able to make out against the present economic order of society, demands a full consideration of all means by which the institution may have a chance of being made to work in a manner more benificial to that large portion of society which at present enjoy the least share of its direct benefit.—*John Stuart Mill.*

WHEN Comrade Smart states that the tendency of trades unions are not in the right direction, that they are not only doing no good but are a hinderance to the labor movement, he makes an assertion not founded on fact. For thirteen years a union man, the writer of this paragraph says from personal knowledge and observation that, the old-time conservatism of trades unions is now but a mere shell, needing only a few more blows to break to pieces. An article in answer to Mr. Smart is promised for our next number.

IN Mediæval Europe almost all land was held from the sovereign on tenure of service, either military or agricultural; and in Great Britain even now, when the services as well as all the reserved rights of the sovereign have long since fallen into disuse or been commuted for taxation, the theory of law does not acknowledge an absolute right of property in land in any individual; the fullest landed proprietor known to the law, the freeholder, is but a "tenant" of the Crown.—*John Stuart Mill.*

The employing of female clerks in large stores and requiring them to stand all day long, for the paltry sum of $4 or $5 a week, deserves the condemnation of all those who have a spark of sympathy for suffering humanity. In conversation with a lady clerk in a large bazaar in Chicago we learned that she received $4 a week, lived nine miles from the store, paid $1.25 car fare and her dinners and suppers took the greater portion of what was left. And still there are people who can see nothing wrong in our present industrial system, a system which forces women into prostitution to get the merest necessaries of life. People should look into this matter and not patronize stores where they will not at least allow their clerks the privilege of sitting while not occupied.

SOME months ago the proprietors of two daily papers in Little Rock, Ark., reduced the wages of their employes 10 per cent., to which the printers acceded. Not satisfied with this, the employers soon after tried to enforce another 10 per cent. reduction. Against this the printers struck. Like sensible persons, they did not stand idle and waste the capital in their Union treasury, but went to work and established a paper and job office of their own; and judging from the appearance of their paper, *The Union*, they are prospering finely. This is the proper way to carry a strike. Now let trades unions inaugurate a system of co-operative funds, so when necessity requires they can employ themselves, and they will have solved the problem of how to successfully conduct strikes.

The French amnesty bill passed the Chamber to take effect July 14.

SUBSCRIBERS AND AGENTS.

We again call your attention to the necessity of being prompt in your payments to THE REVIEW, as it is impossible for us to furnish it gratis, however much we would like to. THE REVIEW is published by three printers, the type being set at odd hours and paper and press work paid out of our pockets with money earned by hard work. We do not propose to make money out of it, as this is a labor of love, but we would like to get the earnest and *substantial* aid of all who wish to have firmly established a magazine that will always devote itself to advocating radical and advanced labor ideas. It is our desire to be as lenient as possible with our patrons, but our means will not allow us to publish a magazine for free distribution. So, come now, comrades, and send along your dues.

TO SECTIONS.

In order to raise money to meet a bill, the Socialistic Tract Association will send their tracts, *postpaid*, to June 10th, for ONE DOLLAR a thousand.

We appeal to all Sections to send an order *immediately*.

JUDSON GRENELL, Sec'y,
116 Howard Street.

SOCIALISTIC LABOR PARTY.

FURNISHED BY THE SECRETARY, PHILIP VAN PATTEN.

NATIONAL EXECUTIVE COMMITTEE.

P. C. Christiansen........128 Antoine st.
Charles Erb...........579 Dequinde st.
Judson Grenell...........116 Howard st.
Gustav Herzig...........29 Napoleon st.
Philip Van Patten.........P. O. Box 597
E. W. Simpson, Rec.Sec'y..90 Wilkins st.
Wm. Kuess.............556 Clinton ave.

General Party News.

On the 13th inst. the Sections of New York, Brooklyn, Jersey City and other neighboring cities united in giving a grand excursion down the bay. Several steamers were needed to accommodate the vast throng, which numbered about 6,000 persons. The affair was one of the most successful ever held by our membership.

Upon the same day as that above mentioned, our Chicago Section gave a picnic at Sharpshooters' Park. Owing to the remoteness of the locality and the failure of the "bus" lines to provide proper facilities, the attendance did not exceed 2,000 persons, but the festival was most successful to all concerned. Able speeches were delivered by Mr. T. W. Taylor, of Pennsylvania, and Mr. Tullis, Greenback delegates to the Convention, who used most radical expressions and declared their endorsement of Socialism. Mr. Taylor is better known as "Old Beeswax," of the *Irish World*. Comrade Morgan reviewed the work of the Convention, and prophesied gratifying results to follow. Dennis Kearney, who promised to speak, failed to put in an appearance, thus disappointing many who had come to hear him. Our Socialist managers are not willing to be held responsible for this failure to carry out the advertised programme, therefore we are in duty bound to vindicate them.

THE CHICAGO CONVENTION.

Report of the Delegates of the Socialistic Labor Party, upon their actions preliminary to, and during their attendance at the National Convention of the Greenback Labor Party at Chicago, June 9th to 11th, 1880.

Preliminary Arrangements.

The National Executive Committee received signed credentials from the Central Committees of the following States: Massachusetts, New York, New Jersey, Pennsylvania, Maryland, Ohio, Indiana, Illinois, Michigan, Wisconsin, Missouri, Kansas and California.

In order to properly select representatives from the Chicago section for those States sending none; also to properly conduct the proceedings at the Convention, in all matters concerning the Party interests, the National Executive Committee elected a Sub-Committee of three, consisting of E. W. Simpson, Judson Grenell and Philip Van Patten, instructed and empowered to represent this Committee in carrying out the instructions adopted by vote of the Party.

On Monday evening, June 7, a joint session of this Sub-Committee, with the State Central Committee of Illinois, was held in Chicago, at 54 W. Lake St., for the purpose of selecting delegates to represent other States, and of transacting such other necessary business as might be legal and proper.

The meeting being called to order by T. J. Morgan, in the name of the Central Committee, he was elected Chairman. After the Party Secretary, Van Patten, had read the instructions by which the Sub-Committee would be guided, the delegates were then entered upon the roll, those sent from other States being placed first in order, and the regular Illinois delegates next, after which proxies to fill out incomplete State delegations were chosen, in the order recommended by the Chicago Section. The delegates then constituted themselves as a body, and elected the following Committee on Programme:

Dr. A. Douai, P. J. McGuire, T. J. Morgan, M. Bachmann, Peter Peterson, W. C. Pollner, John McAuliffe.

This Committee to serve jointly with the Sub-Committee of the National Executive. M. Bachmann read the in-

structions given him by the State Convention of New York, and stated that it had been resolved by that body that only one delegate should represent New York. He would not, however, object to the appointment of nine more delegates, provided they should be bound by the same instructions as himself. It being the sense of the meeting that the instructions adopted by the Party were higher than those of any State, Mr. Bachmann should be authorized to disregard his instructions in so far as they might conflict with those of the Party. The meeting then adjourned, to meet the next morning at 10 o'clock.

Meeting, June 8th, 10 o'clock, A. M. Christian Meier, Chairman. The questions of most importance were then acted upon as follows: that of securing seats in the Greenback Convention, was referred to the Sub-Committee of the National Executive, as was also that of obtaining representation on committees.

A Committee on Credentials, consisting of Bachmann and Schilling, was elected, but after protesting against the decision of the delegates ordering him to disregard his instructions, Bachmann resigned, and the vacancy was filled by the election of Geo. Winter. The meeting then adjourned, the committees being instructed to immediately confer with the proper authorities of the Greenback Party, at the Palmer House.

Conference at Palmer House.

June 8th, 8 o'clock, P. M.

This meeting having been called by the National Executive Committee, through the Associated Press and the Labor newspapers of the whole country, was called to order by the Party Secretary, Van Patten, who stated the object of the Conference. T. J. Morgan was elected chairman, the minutes being kept by the Party Secretary. It was resolved to hold a public meeting for one hour, and then proceed in Executive Session.

Dr. Douai and C. Meier were delegated to serve with the Sub-Committee of the National Executive, all of whom then withdrew to confer with the National Committee of the Greenback Party.

The chair then invited delegates of other organizations to speak. Mr. A. F. Carpenter, delegate of the Greenback Party from Illinois, spoke in the interest of harmony and unity, as the cause is a common one. Mrs. J. R. Stone, of Boston, and George Schilling, of Chicago, Socialist delegates, spoke in the same strain, followed by Mr. Brown, a Greenback delegate from Missouri; T. J. Morgan and John McAuliffe, Socialists; Mr. Bartlett, of the Union Greenback Party of Illinois; and Dr. A. Douai and P. J. McGuire, Socialist delegates from New Jersey and Missouri, respectively. All of the speeches were tempered with wisdom and moderation, those of the Greenback delegates expressing pleasure at the steps taken by the Socialists; and those of the latter, declaring a firm determination to procure a sound Labor platform and reliable candidates, as a condition of our support. The meeting then adjourned as a public gathering, and the Socialist delegates, about eighty in number, went into an executive session. After roll-call, it was resolved, that as no objections against Chicago delegates had been sustained by parties raising the same, all disabilities should be removed, and the full delegation recognized as legal.

The Party Secretary then reported that the conference held by the Sub-Committee and associate delegates jointly with the National Committee of the Greenback Party, had resulted in the adoption by the latter of a resolution recommending to the Convention the admission of the Socialist delegates. Also, that the New Jersey delegates had unanimously resolved to recommend the admission of fifty Socialist delegates, three of whom should serve upon the Committee on Platform and Resolutions. The report was received.

P. J. McGuire, for the Committee on plan of operations reported—

1st. The election of Schilling and Winter as Committee on Credentials.

2d. Recommendation that all delegates should be bound by the resolutions of this Confer-nce. (This was further amended, to read "and the

seven shall be the authorized speakers for the Socialists in the Convention.

The following four names were added to this list of speakers:

Mrs. J. R. Stone, O. A. Bishop, A. R. Parsons and Christian Meier. Mr. Meier withdrew his name.

7th. That none shall speak other than those selected, except by permission given by majority vote of our delegation.

The above recommendations were all adopted.

Dr. Douai then moved that the Committee on Platform should be instructed to work for the adoption of the following planks of the Platform of the Socialistic Labor Party, namely: 1, 2, 3. 6, 7, and 9, of *National Demands*, and 1, 2, 3, 4, 5, 6, 7, and 10 of *State Demands*. The motion was adopted. O. A. Bishop then stated that the entire Illinois delegation of the Greenback Party had voted in favor of admitting the Socialist delegates to full rights in the Convention.

The meeting then adjourned to meet again on the following day at 10 o'clock A. M. Agreeable to the above resolution, the delegates assembled at the time appointed, and were supplied with their credentials. The Committees being unable to work until the Convention should become organized, had no reports to make, therefore shortly after twelve o'clock at noon, the delegates marched in a body to the Convention and took seats in the gallery.

The Convention.

The Convention formed its temporary organization by the election of G. De La Matyr as chairman and Chas. H. Litchman as secretary.

Contrary to the usual rule the Committee, which can only be legally elected by the permanent convention, were then chosen by this temporary organization, (a body which has the right to elect only the Committee on Credentials). The Convention then adjourned and the Committees held their sessions

of the Committees were ready to report. Able speeches strongly tinged with socialism were made by Messrs Wallace and Wright, representing the currency reformers of Canada, and by Dennis Kearney, the California agitator.

At 10:30 o'clock, next morning, June 10th, the Convention was called to order, and proceeded to form permanent organization.

The Committee on Credentials reported in favor of admitting forty-four Socialistic delegates, only six of whom were to be from the State of Illinois. The committee also reported favorably on credentials from the following Labor Organizations: Social Political Workingmen's Society of Chicago, (1 delegate); Chicago Workingwomen's Union, (3 delegates); Workingmen's Party, of Kansas, (3 delegates); Eight-Hour League, of Chicago, (6 delegates); Union Greenback Labor Party (Pomeroy Clubs, 187 delegates). The Committee accompanied the above report with resolutions recommending that no State should be allowed to increase its vote by the admission of the delegates of other organizations, and that the accredited delegates from each State be authorized to cast the full vote of such State, to which it is entitled under the call for the Convention. These resolutions would have the effect of disfranchising the Socialists and all other delegates coming under the same conditions, and a long and excited debate commenced.

Secretary Litchman read the following

MINORITY REPORT.

"We dissent from so much of the majority report as permits the entire vote of a State to be cast by less than a full delegation We therefore respectfully submit the following: That each State shall be entitled only to so many votes in the Convention as there are actually delegates present and duly accredited from said State; and that the delegates from the Social Labor Party vote by themselves as a separate body."

More confusion and excited discussion followed, and the question being put on the first portion of the minority report, relating to the right of a State delegation, regardless of numbers, to cast the full vote to which the State is entitled under the call, the adverse recommendation was *lost*. That portion of the majority report referring to the regular delegates, was then adopted.

The question then remained unsettled as to admission of delegates from other organizations that had not conformed to the call.

Our Socialist delegates then submitted the following

MEMORIAL.

To the National Convention of the Greenback Party:

We, the undersigned representatives of the Socialistic Labor Party, duly authorised by our full delegation, present the following memorial to your body, and hope for its favorable consideration. We desire seats in your Convention as a body, for the reason that we have cast nearly 100,000 votes, and that, as a body we could not come under the call that brought this Convention together. We desire to unite our forces with yours, to make common cause against the common enemy—the *Money Power*. We ask the right to participate in your deliberations, and rather than be divided among the State delegations, we will surrender our right to vote on the question of Presidential nominees.

For the delegation:

PHILIP VAN PATTEN,
National Secretary.
DR. A. DOUAI,

The memorial caused another noisy debate, in which Comrades Morgan and Van Patten explained the position of our Party to the satisfaction of the Convention, which then adopted a special resolution to admit the Socialists as a separate body, with full right to vote, as follows:

The Socialist delegates to the number of forty-four, no more than six of whom shall belong to the State of Illinois, we recommend be admitted to seats in the Convention as full delegates.

It was then resolved to admit the Union Greenback delegates under the provisions of the majority report, and these soon arrived with a band of music, amid great enthusiasm and rejoicing.

Permanent organization was then effected by the election of Mr. Richard F. Trevellick, of Michigan, chairman; Chas. H. Litchman, Secretary; George Godfrey, James W. Muffly, J. H. Randall, M. M. McLeod, L. A. Wood, Philip Van Patten, Perry B. Maxson, W. L. Hope, T. V. Powderly, and C. H. Roberts, Assistant Secretaries.

The list of Socialistic delegates is as follows:

New Jersey—Dr. A. Douai.
California—Philip Van Patten, John Paulson.
Michigan—E. W. Simpson, Judson Grenell, Jos. A. Labadie, N. L. Barlow.
Massachusetts—Mrs. Josephine R. Stone.
Ohio—W. C. Pollner.
Missouri—P. J. McGuire, George Winter, Enoch Berger, Julius Gerber, R. Lorenz, M. Schalk.
New York—M. Bachmann, J. J. Altpeter, Geo. Sloan, Geo. Gaide, J. C. Warner, Peter Peterson, Paul Ehmann.
Pennsylvania—C. Loether, John McAuliffe, O. A. Bishop, Wm. Bluhm, Jas. White, Alfred Gould, R. Beck.
Indiana—John F. Brown.
Wisconsin—M. Biron (sub. Christian Steger,) E. Strassmann, Thos Bucklin. J. Graumann.
Illinois—Christian Meier, F. Bielefeldt, T. J. Morgan, G. A. Schilling, Frank Stauber, Mrs. A. R. Parsons.

Kansas—E. A. Stevens, Albert Florus, J. Fossell, Thomas Ryan.

After a number of congratulatory speeches by representatives of the Union Greenback Party, the Women's Suffrage Association, etc., the Convention adjourned.

At 8 o'clock in the evening the session was reopened, and the Committee on Platform reported the following

PLATFORM.

Civil Government should guarantee the divine right of every laborer to the results of his toil, thus enabling the producers of wealth to provide themselves with the means for physical comfort, and the facilities for mental, social, and moral culture ; and we condemn as unworthy of our civilization the barbarism which imposes upon the wealth-producers a state of perpetual drudgery as the price of bare animal existence.

Notwithstanding the enormous increase of productive power, the universal introduction of labor-saving machinery, and the discovery of new agents for the increase of wealth, the task of the laborer is scarcely lightened, the hours of toil are but little shortened, and few producers are lifted from poverty into comfort and pecuniary independence.

The associated monopolies, the international syndicates and other income classes demand dear money and cheap labor, a "strong government" and hence a weak people.

Corporate control of the volume of money has been the means of dividing society into two classes ; of the unjust distribution of the products of labor, and of building up monopolies of associated capital, endowed with power to confiscate private property. It has kept money scarce, and scarcity of money enforces debt trade, and public and corporate loans—debt engenders usury, and usury ends in the bankruptcy of the borrower. Other results are deranged markets, uncertainty in manufacturing enterprise and agriculture, precarious and intermittent employment for the laborer, industrial war increasing pauperism and crime, and the consequent intimidation and disfranchisement of the producer, and a rapid declination into corporate feudalism.

Therefore, we declare :

1. That the right to make and issue money is a sovereign power to be maintained by the people for the common benefit. The delegation of this right to corporations is a surrender of the central attribute of sovereignty, void of constitutional sanction, conferring upon a subordinate irresponsible power, absolute dominion over industry and commerce. All money, whether metallic or paper, should be issued and its volume controlled by the government, and not by or through banking corporations, and when so issued should be a full legal tender for all debts public and private.

2. That the bonds of the United States should not be refunded, but paid as rapidly as is practicable according to contract. To enable the government to meet these obligations, legal-tender currency should be substituted for the notes of the national banks, the national banking system abolished, and the unlimited coinage of silver as well as gold established by law.

3. That labor should be so protected by national and state authority as to equalize its burdens and insure a just distribution of its results ; the eight-

hour law of congress should be enforced; the sanitary condition of industrial establishments placed under rigid control; the competition of contract convict labor abolished ; a bureau of labor statistics established; factories, mines and workshops inspected; the employment of children under 14 years of age forbidden, and wages paid in cash.

4. Slavery being simply cheap labor, and cheap labor being simply slavery, the importation and presence of Chinese serfs necessarily tends to brutalize and degrade American labor: therefore, immediate steps should be taken to abrogate the Burlingame treaty.

5. Railroad land grants forfeited by reason of non-fulfillment of contract, should be immediately reclaimed by the government; and henceforth the public domain reserved exclusively as homes for actual settlers.

6. It is the duty of congress to regulate interstate commerce, all lines of communication and transportation should be brought under such legislative control as shall secure moderate, fair and uniform rates for passenger and freight traffic.

7 We denounce as destructive to prosperity and dangerous to liberty, the action of the old parties in fostering and sustaining gigantic land, railroad and money corporations and monopolies, invested with, and exercising powers belonging to the government, and yet not responsible to it for the manner of their exercise.

8. That the constitution in giving congress the power to borrow money, and in time of war to raise and support armies, to provide and maintain a navy, never intended that the men who loaned their money for an interest consideration should be preferred to the soldier and sailor who periled their lives and shed their blood on land and sea in defence of their country, and we condemn the cruel class legislation of the republican party, which, while professing great gratitude to the soldier, has most unjustly discriminated against him and in favor of the bondholder.

9. All property should bear its just proportion of taxation, and we demand a graduated income tax.

10. We denounce as most dangerous the efforts everywhere manifest to restrict the right of suffrage.

11. We are opposed to an increase of the standing army in time of peace, and the insidious scheme to establish an enormous military power under the guise of militia laws.

12. We demand absolute democratic rules for the government of congress, placing all representatives of the people upon an equal footing, and taking away from committees a veto power greater than that of the president.

13. We demand a government of the people, by the people, and for the people, instead of a government of the bondholder, by the bondholder, and for the bondholder ; and we denounce every attempt to stir up sectional strife as an effort to conceal monstrous crimes against the people.

14. In the furtherance of these ends we ask the co-operation of all fair-minded people. We have no quarrel with individuals, wage no war upon classes, but upon vicious institutions. We are not content to endure further discipline from our present actual rulers, who, having dominion over money, over transportation, over land and labor, and largely over the press and the machinery of government, wield unwarrantable power over our institutions, and over life and property.

The report was adopted without debate, on a call for the previous question.

A number of additional planks were offered for insertion in the Platform, upon the subject of mortgaged real estate,

woman's suffrage, etc., and the Socialists presented the following: We
declare that Land, Light, Air and Water
are the free gifts of nature to all mankind, and any law or custom of Society
that allows any person to monopolize
more of these gifts than he has a right to,
to the detriment of the rights of others,
we earnestly condemn and seek to abolish. Comrade T. J. Morgan, the author
of this resolution, obtained the floor and
in a short speech of ten minutes, advocated its adoption. The speech was well
received, and the resolution was referred
to the Committee on Platform and Resolutions. A resolution on woman's suffrage was also read, and after much discussion the Convention proceeded to
vote on this, as the Committee had
reported favorably within the last few
minutes, although no mention was made
by the Committee, of the Socialist resolution. The roll-call being taken upon
the woman's suffrage plank, the Secretary, after the States had voted, called
for the vote of the Social Labor delegates. It was announced to be 42 in
the affirmative and 2 negative. Several
Greenback delegates then objected to
allowing the Socialists the right to vote
as a separate body. Great confusion
commenced and upon appeal being
made to the chair, he ordered the reading of the resolution by which the Socialists had been admitted. The Secretary
read several resolutions, but not the
proper one, and the chair decided that
the majority report of the Committee
on Credentials had stated that by the
admission of delegates from other organizations, the vote of no State could be
increased. The Socialists protested that
they had been admitted as a separate
body, and did not vote with any State
delegation. The chair maintained his
ruling and the Socialists, after several
struggles to secure the adoption of the
land resolution, left the Convention at
about midnight, The Convention went
on with the nominations for President
and Vice-President, resulting in the

mit to your body our grievances. After having
been admitted to the full rights of delegates, we
were deprived of our vote on Woman's Suffrage—
a question totally foreign to that of Presidential
nominations. In the interest of the people we
presented a plank on the Land Question, to be
placed in the Platform. This plank was referred
to a committee with instructions to report upon it
at once, and to bring it before the Convention for
its action. The committee failed to report, and
instead of calling for that report, in answer to our
repeated requests, the Convention went into nominations for President, thus evading the duty of
placing themselves on record upon the Land
Question. Under these circumstances we feel it
our duty to again demand that this plank on the
Land Question be called up for the action of the
Convention, and in case this is refused we shall, to
our great regret, be compelled to withdraw from
the Convention and leave it to our constituents to
decide what is to be done.

A motion was then made and carried
to adopt the Socialists' land resolution.
The Convention then adjourned.

Final Resolutions.

At eleven o'clock a. m. the Socialist
delegates assembled at 54 West Lake
street, and adopted the following resolutions:
1st, That, in our judgment, the Socialists have every reason to be satisfied
with the result of the Convention.
2d. That we recommend to the Sections throughout the land that they
work hand in hand with the Greenbackers in the Presidential campaign,
and make the best possible use of this
splendid opportunity for making known
our principles.
3d. That while we thus co-operate
with the Greenback Labor Party, we
still maintain our separate organization.
4th. That in case the National Committee of the Greenback Labor Party
crowd out or ignore the resolution relating to the Land Question, which had
been adopted by the Convention, we
will still support the Greenback candidates, (as the Platform is full of Socialism,) but will publish in the *Irish World*
an inquiry addressed to the National
Committee, and should they seek to ex-

struggled in behalf of our delegates in the Convention.

6th. That the Sub-Committee of the National Executive Committee is instructed to publish a correct record of the actions of the Socialist delegates at this Convention, and all necessary information to the Party, in the LABOR REVIEW and all Party papers.

Respectfully submitted,

E. W. SIMPSON,
JUDSON GRENELL,
PHILIP VAN PATTEN,

Sub-Committee of the Nat. Executive Com.

Detroit, June 15th, 1880.

SOCIALISTIC LABOR PARTY.

. Call for a General Party Vote.

The Sections will hold special meetings, properly announced, for the purpose of taking the votes of all members upon the questions stated below.

Sections having a number of branches and represented by a central committee, will take the vote by branches, and the central committee will report to us the vote of those branches, as well as the total result. All reports must be sent to the National Executive Committee on or before August 1st, 1880.

Question 1st.—Shall our Party support during the coming Presidential campaign, the candidates of the Greenback Labor Party, namely—

Jas. B. Weaver, of Iowa, for President.

B. J. Chambers, of Texas, for Vice-President.

Question 2nd. — Does the Platform adopted by the National Convention at Chicago, on June 10th, 1880, meet with the endorsement of the Socialistic Labor Party as one upon which all labor elements can combine against the common enemy?

The exact number of votes in the affirmative and negative must be accurately reported. The report of the Socialistic delegates should be officially read in every Section meeting when the vote is taken.

THE NATIONAL EX. COM.

PHILIP VAN PATTEN,
Secretary.

CONVENTION NOTES.

Mrs. J. R. Stone, of the Boston Section, was a power in the Massachusetts delegation.

The Greenback delegates publicly declared that at least two-thirds of their number were Socialists in conviction.

The Platform demands (plank 3,) "That labor should be so protected by National and State authority as to equalize its burdens and insure a just distribution of its results." What more can Socialists ask? Our land resolution was adopted too late for incorporation in the Platform, but we can afford to lose it in view of the radical demands already in that document.

We will by no means give up our separate organization nor our radical position, but we can simply declare that our Party *endorses* the candidates and platform chosen by the Greenback Labor Convention, and will work for them in our own way.

Financial Report of the National Executive Committee, for May.

RECEIPTS:

Albany Section, dues, - - -	$2 40
Louisville, H. Moormann, pamphlets, - - - - -	2 00
St. Louis Section, dues, -	25 00
Cleveland Section, dues, - -	3 80
Brooklyn, N. Y. Section, dues, -	15 00
Hoboken, N. J. Section, dues, -	2 50
Buffalo, N.Y., Convention reports,	2 50
San Francisco Section, dues, -	6 75
Monongahela, Pa., Wm. Menge,	50
Leadville, Col., C. J. Hildreth, -	10
New York, H. Nitzsche, for Bulletin, - - - - - -	2 34
Secretary Van Patten, pamphlets,	35
Accounts due Bulletin, - -	1 00
Chicago Section, dues, - -	12 15
W. Hoboken Section, dues,	1 80
Rockville, Conn., - - -	3 30
Paterson, N.J., Section, dues, -	10 00
St. Joseph, Mo., Section, dues, -	1 60
	93 09
Balance at last report, - -	92 11
	$185 20

EXPENDITURES:

Current expenses, postage, printing, etc., - - - - -	$78 53
Salary of Secretary, four weeks,	48 00
	$126 53
Balance, cash on hand, - -	58 77

THE LABOR REVIEW.

Vol. 1. No. 7 DETROIT, MICH., JULY, 1880. PRICE SEVEN CENTS.

THE LABOR REVIEW.

TERMS OF SUBSCRIPTION.

One year, in advance, - - 75 cents
Six months, in advance, - - 40 cents
Three months, in advance, - 20 cents
Single copies, - - - - 7 cents

☞Five copies to one address, in advance, $3.00.

☞ Terms to Agents, four cents per copy. Agents must make returns by the first of each month, and also stating how many copies are needed.

☞Three cent postage-stamps taken for fractional parts of a dollar.

☞An Agent wanted in every town in the United States to canvass for this journal.

☞ When a subscription has expired, the subscriber will be notified, and if he does not renew before the next number is issued, his name will be dropped from the list. Address,

CO-OPERATING PRINTERS,

121 Porter street, Detroit, Mich.

What Socialism Means.

I have been greatly pleased with the extracts of socialism published in the May number of THE REVIEW. It is pleasing to find a lady so imbued with the socialistic spirit, and of so nice analytical discrimination. I hope we shall hear from Lizzie Denton Seybold often.

Perhaps she will pardon me, however, if in the interest of our cause I venture to suggest some half dozen amendments to her not less than 38 articles of socialism. My suggestions are intended solely to stimulate thought and to promote harmony of opinion among Socialists.

1 It means that money will be simply the worker's draft on the national deposits for value received in labor, and will no longer be used as capital.

2. It means that the time of all men will be valuable in proportion to service, and will be paid for according to its value.

3. It means that no man shall own an acre of land, but the people as a whole shall control the land and all other natural resources.

4. It means that the individual occupancy of land and houses will only be for individual uses.

5. It means that all small farms will pass away, and that the people will live in individual homes or co-operative homes, according to individual preference.

6. It means that the best provision will exist against orphanage, sickness, accident and death by a national system of insurance, to which all will contribute by means of a national fund.

7. It means that there will be no distinctions between men and women in regard to civil, political or any other rights or opportunities.

With these amendments to the articles to which they refer, I can endorse the whole list as published in May.

L. D. S. has started a good plan of mutual criticism which will help to bring us all thinking together. In unity there is strength, and there can be no real unity without harmony. Variety, however, is not inconsistent with harmony; only that kind that produces discord.

W. G. H. SMART.

Labor Reform.

The term Labor Reform, although rather vague in its analysis, has become by common usage to characterize the objective points of those who, impressed with the extreme badness of present social institutions, as shown by the monstrous—the unprecedented—robbery of the producing classes on the one hand, and the equally monstrous and unprecedented endowment of the parasitic on the other, seek to relieve the former and to curb the latter.

Briefly stated, it is an inspiration and demand for equitable distribution of the products of labor.

The discussion of this matter, and other entanglements which constantly crush, strangle, murder and devour humanity, is logically and sharply divisible into two parts, viz:

1st. How did labor get into the trap?

2d. How will it get out of it?

Adam Smith—an authority more quoted by the dangerous and parasitic classes than any other writer—honestly and justly answers the first query in the first chapter of his "Wealth of Nations," thus:

"The produce of labor constitutes the natural recompense or wages of labor.

"In that original state of things which precedes both the appropriation of land and the accumulation of stock the whole proceeds of labor belongs to the laborer.

"He has neither landlord nor master to share with him.

"Had this state continued the wages of labor would have augmented with all these improvements in its productive powers to which the division of labor gives occasion.

"All things would gradually have cheapened. They would have been produced by a smaller quantity of labor, and as the commodities produced by equal quantities of labor would naturally in this state of things be exchanged for one another, they would have been purchased likewise with the produce of smaller quantity.

"But this original state of things in which the laborer enjoyed the whole produce of his own labor, could not last beyond the first introduction of the appropriation of land and the accumulation of stock."

Mr. Smith properly couples the appropriation of land and the accumulation of stock as the initial steps; the conditions precedent for the robbery of the producing classes. It would, however, be an insult to Mr. Smith's common sense to suppose that a mere accumulation of stock could be so calamitous. Such accumulation of stock is devastative only by enabling the more avaricious, from the amplitude of their resources, to plunder the less provident by exhaustive and usurious exactions for advances to relieve their pressing necessities.

The basic causes are therefore sublimited and epitomized in four words:

LAND MONOPOLY AND USURY.

Adam Smith was not the first to proclaim these truths. They have been reiterated withour ceasing from the days of Moses until now by every political economist worthy of the name.

In the earlier history of the race these most devilish elements of oppression were upheld by their possessors by the brute elements of physical force. Since the advent of gunpowder which placed prince and peasant on a physical level, diplomacy and legislation have been the less demonstrative but more effective agencies.

A recent special commissioner of the United States ably said in this connection:—

"The unproductives are still animated by their ancient spirit, and being the chief makers of the laws and institutions for the protection of labor and ingenuity the increase of products and the exchange and transfer of property, they shape all their devices so cunningly and work them so cleverly that they—the non-producers—continue to grow richer faster than the producers.

"In short, the ancient combat, old as the dawn of civilization, still goes on animated on the one side by the desire to keep, and on the other by the desire to get, the producers combining rather blindly and clumsily against the schemes of the unproductives as they combined in successive stages in all past history against violence, robbery, plunder, theft, fraud and the grosser acts whereby property was transferred from the hands of the many into those of the few."

How this control of the "makers of laws and institutions for the protection of labor," adverted to by the commissioner, was obtained is clearly shown by the classification made by Moses W. Field when he was a Member of Congress a few years since, of the make-up of the Lower House in which he was a member from Michigan, thus:

Six lumbermen, 13 boss manufacturers, 7 doctors, 14 merchants, 13 farmers, 3 millers, 1 mechanic, 100 lawyers, 189 bankers, 1 minister, 1 land surveyor, 1 barber, 1 professor; total, 350.

When barbarism was superseded by civilization the robber classes became more exacting in their demands and servile legislatures added to their previous abrogation of sovereignty over the lands of the nation the delegation of the control of the national prerogatives of the control of the people's highways and the people's moneys.

From the above it will be seen that while the producers, say the farmers, mechanics, millers and lumbermen, laboring men—at least 80 per cent. of the voters and taxpayers of the country, have but 33 representatives, or less than 10 per cent. of representation; the bankers, and their jackals the lawyers, who probably do not form over 1 per cent. of the population, have 80 per cent. of representation, thus curiously reversing the equities of the matter, thus: Producers entitled to 80 per cent. have 10; Usurers entitled to 1 per cent. have 80. In this connection the atrocity of the capture of the government by the miserable minority of 1 per cent. of parasites, is not as culpable as the unparalelled imbecility of the overwhelming major-

ity of 80 per cent. of the producers in permitting it.

Able writers have of late with graphic power imagined a coming dictatorship which should institute the titles, powers, and paraphernalia of European monarchs and notabilities, but their wildest dreams have fallen short of the usurpations which the insiduous wiles of Robber and Imperial legislation have fastened upon us.

In a word, by the sovereign endowments which treasonable congresses have conferred upon the rapacious vampires of

Land speculators,
Usurous blood-suckers,
National Banks absorptionists,
Railroad pirates, and
Bullion bull-dozers,

it is no exageration to say that no dictator, even though incarnating the fiendishness of Nero or Caligula, or both, could have inflicted the devastation which has in the past been inaugurated, developed, sustained, and intensified by the vice-regal authority of the above named and other privileged and endowed beneficiaries and banditti.

WHAT ARE YOU GOING TO DO ABOUT IT?

The common sense response is: Retrace the steps which have plunged this republic into this quagmire; repeal the legislation which is the creative source of all woes, and then make this government in practice what Jefferson declared it should be—one "of the people, BY the people and FOR the people." Let the producing classes read, study, educate and combine.

Learn and teach first this primary lesson, that all honest differences of opinion are caused by lack of intelligence, and that if all were educated, there would be no more diversity of conviction than there now is as to the orthodoxy of the multiplication table.

A few centuries ago the scientific and religious world were divided in angry discusion as to whether the earth revolved around the sun or the reverse. Now but one opinion prevails.

Most people concentrate their attention upon one simple and partial reform—*good*, NEEDED—INDISPENSABLE it may be, but unsustained by kindred support, powerless to stand alone. Some folks press so closely to their mind's eye the traditional six-pence that it hides the available dollar; they treat the advocates of germain reform as tresspassers and interlopers; they seem to arrogate to themselves infalibility of judgement and to deny to others the possession of even common sense, they transform themselves into human hedge-hogs in their special pleadings, ironclad against all receptivity and bristling with elements of offense.

As like produces like in the social and intellectual as fully as in material spheres, this assumption of superior wisdom, this utter absence of Christian charity, tends to transform those who should be a co-operative and harmonious family, into a pack of antagonistic and quarrelsome wolves. It may be said, and truly said, that this terrible curse of individual self-righteousness is fast abating, and that the several columns of the army of humanity are rapidly being concentrated against the whole line; the numerous batteries of the common enemy. Granted, but life is short. Crowds of men, women and children are daily, hourly and momentarily sacrificed to the hideous idols of societary abuses, more exhaustive in their exactions. more de-

The crown of martyrdom is a good thing, but the glory of victory in a just cause is better. Moses' position standing on Mount Pisgah in full view of the promised land, whose bounties he was never to enjoy, was not so satisfactory as that Washington gladdened in his declining years by the rich harvest of blessings—the fruits of his earlier labors and persistent work.

JOHN G. DREW. ·

To a Poor Man.

"Poor" man, working your ten hours a day for so many weary years, do you not wonder how it happens that you are poor, who do so much, while the men in the next street are rich, who do little or nothing?

You cannot help being poor so long as the usages of society take from you more than half your earnings, for the support of that aristocratic crowd of social parasites known as bankers, bond-holders, money-lenders, railroad magnates, speculators, landlords, and other useless classes. Don't you see where your shoe pinches?

Perhaps you are so blind as to think that the rich man is a benefit to you, because he "gives you work." Does he employ you for your benefit? Nothing of the kind. For every dollar he gives you in the shape of wages, he expects to reap another as profits in some shape. And these profits from your labor, whether in the shape of interest, rent or profits, stare you in the face every day, as you go to work, and

reorganization of society as will prevent their getting any more of it!

What right have these "upper" classes to absorb the whole surplus of wealth created by labor? None whatever. No better right than the highwayman has to stop you in the street, and demand half your money. You are robbed in a "genteel" manner, and not put in fear of your life. That is all the difference. You are plundered without power to help yourself.

All this must be changed. The present social system makes you a serf, not only for a few years but for generations. The wealth of society has always come from the servitude of labor. It is a hereditary bondman everywhere, alike in monarchies, aristocracies and republics.

The wage-workers of all grades constitute two-thirds of the nation. But they have no idea of a proper remedy for their wrongs, and no cohesion, and are therefore twisted and turned, cheated and robbed, kicked and abused by the other third. Now, what they ought to do depends upon what they desire. If they wish to become their own employers, and enjoy the whole fruits of their labor, they must consolidate themselves into one vast organization of wage-workers, and proclaim to the world their determination to secure industrial liberty, and put an end to the tyranny and exactions of capital.

How shall they accomplish this end?

1. They can effect it indirectly through political action, by obtaining control of the National and State governments, thereby having power to legislate as they see fit; or,

2. They can bring their organized power to bear directly on capital in every factory, and workshop, and on every railroad, demanding *partnership* and an equitable share of their earnings in addition to their

It ought to be very easy for a wage-worker to make up his mind what he will do. It is for him to decide whether he will be free or continue a slave, with all the poverty, low wages, overwork and misery that is the portion of unowned slaves. A foundation for this grand consolidation of labor exists in almost every state, and is the only one devoted to industrial reforms and the rights of labor. Its success will put an end to all the wrongs of labor, social and political. It will change our political government into one devoted to industrial matters, in which the party politician can have no place. No man can set bounds to the great reforms that will naturally grow out of a reconstruction of society based on the independence and self-government of labor—meaning thereby not an empty vote for a change of despotisms, as now, but a perfect industrial liberty, fraternity and equality.

If you work for your living, then a genuine labor-party is your party. Your remedy lies in those industrial reforms represented by what is termed Socialism. Look at its principles thoroughly, listen to its orators, read its papers and tracts, and you will soon discover whether or not it represents your desires and interests. You must make some sacrifices to help yourself. Socialism is unrepresented, outlawed by capital and its hirelings, because it represents an aggressive labor-party. It dares to ask for its rights. It dares to ask for industial liberty. It has come into the world to put an end to the conflict between capital and labor forever.   J. F. Bray.

MANUFACTURING and commercial systems have so remorselessly plundered labor, and our perverse social system generated so many antagonisms between individuals and classes, that it is hard to find a healthy

Examine This.

No president or senate should have the appointing power. It gives them a power inconsistent with democratic institutions. It is for the people to elect. The office of a $50,-000 president should be done away with and an executive committee take its place. Then the Senate, which is unnecessary and obstructive to the people's will, should be abolished, the House of Representatives being quite sufficient for the drafting of all necessary laws, which must come before the people direct for approval. These needed reforms are essential to the success of this or any republic, for they will do away with that one man, or one class power, the monarchical idea, which, under present forms, still exists, very inconsistently with democratic principles. Let the American people, to whom the whole world looks for the success of democratic principles, remember that the words of Patrick Henry, "Eternal vigilance is the price of liberty," are not a mere empty phrase, but a fact taught by the experience of those who have lived and died for it, and they should examine carefully the platforms and principles of the different parties now in the field, and act only with that one which advocates true democratic principles.   McN.

WHAT a difference it does make whose ox is gored. A combination on the part of manufacturers to raise the price of their goods by restricting production is hailed as "a step in the right direction." But if mechanics combine to raise the value of their labor by restricting competition it is denounced as unlawful.

WHILE it is not within the power of any one ruler or one employer to change present societary conditions, yet as upholders of injustice they are deserving of all the condemnation that can be heaped upon them.

THE CONVICT.

CHAPTER VII.

The Thenardiers, being irregulary paid, constantly wrote her letters, whose contents afflicted her, and postage ruined her. One day they wrote her that little Cosette was quite naked, that she wanted a flannel skirt, and that the mother must send at least ten francs for the purpose. She crumped the letter in her hands all day, and at night-fall went to a barber's at the corner of the street, and removed her comb. Her splendid light hair fell down to her hips.

"What fine hair!" the barber exclamed.

"What will you give for it?" she asked.

"Ten francs."

"Cut it off."

She bought a skirt and sent it to the Thenardiers; it made them furious for they wanted the money. They gave it to Eponine, and the poor lark continued to shiver. Fantine thought: "My poor child is no longer cold, for I have dressed her in my hair." She wore small round caps which hid her shorn head, and she still looked pretty in them.

One day she received from the Thenardiers a letter to the following effect: "Cosette is ill with a miliary fever. She must have expensive drugs, and that ruins us, and we cannot pay for them any longer. If you do not send us forty francs within a week, the little one will be dead."

She became thoughtful and sat down to her work. At the end of a quarter of an hour she asked, "Do you know what a military fever is?"

"Yes, it is an illness."

"Does it require much medicine?"

"Oh, an awful lot."

"Does it attack children?"

"More than anybody."

"Do they die of it?"

"Plenty," said Marguerite.

Fantine read the letter once again.

At night, she went out and could be seen proceeding in the direction of the Rue de Paris.

The next morning Marguerite said, "What is the matter with you, Fantine?"

"Nothing," the girl said, "I am all right. My child will not die of that frightful disease for want of assistance, and I am satisfied."

As she said this, she pointed to two Napoleons that glistened on the table.

"Oh! Lord," said Marguerite, "why 'tis a fortune; wherever did you get them from?"

"I had them by me," Fantine answered.

At the same time she smiled, and it was a fearful smile. A reddish saliva stained the corners of her lips, and she had a black hole in her mouth—two teeth were pulled out. Her eyes were very bright, and she felt a settled pain at the top of her left shoulder-blade, while she coughed frequently.

She deeply hated Father Madeleine, and sewed for seventeen hours a day; but a speculator hired all the female prisoners and reduced the prices of the free workmen to nine sous a day. Seventeen hours' work for nine sous! About the same time Thenardier wrote to her that unless he received one hundred francs at once, he would turn poor Cosette, who had scarce recovered, out of doors, into the cold, and must do what she could or rot.

And the unfortunate girl went on the streets.

* * * * *

Eight or ten months after the events we have described in the previous chapter, on a night when snow had fallen, a dandy was amusing himself by annoying a creature, who was prowling about in a low-necked ball dress and with flowers in her hair, before the windows of the officers' cafe. This creature was Fantine. The dandy, to still further annoy her, came behind her and threw a handful of snow down her back. With a yell of rage Fantine turned on him and dug her nails into his face.

An officer immediately appeared and of course arrested the innocent party—Fantine—and brought her before the police officer.

On entering Fantine crouched down motionless in a corner like a frightened dog. Women of this class are by the French laws left entirely to the discretion of the police.

A prostitute had assaulted a citizen and he, Javert, had witnessed it, he turned to Fantine: "You will have six months for it."

The wretched girl started.

"Six months, six months' imprisonment!" she cried.

"Said Javert, "I have listened to you. Have you said all? be off, now, you have six months. The Eternal Father in person could not alter it."

"Wait a minute, if you please."

Javert raised his eyes, and recognized M. Madeleine; he took off his hat and bowed with a sort of vexed awkwardness.

"I beg your pardon, M. le Marie——"

The words "le Marie" produced a strange effect on Fantine; she sprang up like a spectre emerging from the ground, thrust back the soldiers, walked straight up to M. Madeleine before she could be prevented, and looking at him wildly, she exclaimed:

"So you are the Mayor!"

Then she burst into a laugh and spat in his face. M. Madeleine wiped his face and said:

"Inspector Javert, set this woman at liberty."

"At liberty! I am to be let go! I shall not be sent to prison for six months!"

"Sergeant," shouted Javert, "do you not see that the wench is bolt-

ing? Who told you to let her go?"
"I did," said Madeleine.

Javeret objected.

"But, Monsieur le Maire——"

"Permit me sir——"

"Not a word!"

"Still——"

"Leave the room!" said M. Madeleine. Javert received the blow right in his chest, like a Russian soldier; he bowed down to the ground to the Mayor, and went out. Fantine stood up against the door, and watched him pass by her in stupor. She had seen two men struggling in her presance, who held in their hands her liberty, her life, her soul, her child. One of these men dragged her towards the gloom, the other restored her to the light. In this struggle, which she gazed at through the exaggeration of terror, the two men seemed to her giants; one spoke like a demon, the other like her good angel. The angel had vanquished the. demon, and the thing which made her shudder from head to foot was that this angel, this · liberator, was the man whom she abhorred, the Mayor whom she had so long. regarded as the cause of all her woes; and at the very moment when she had insulted him in such a hideous way, he saved her.

"I have heard your story. I know nothing about what you have said, but I believe, I feel that it is true. I was even ignorant that you had left the factory, but why did you not apply to me? This is what I will do for you; I will pay your debts and send for your child, or you can go to it. You can live here, in Paris, or wherever you please, and I will provide for your child and yourself. I will give you all the money you require, and you will become respectable again in becoming happy, and I will say no more than that: if all be as you say, and I do not doubt it, you have never

ceased to be virtuous in the sight of God! Poor woman."

This was more than poor Fantine could endure. To have her Cosette! to leave this infamous life! to live free, rich, happy, and respectable with Cosette! to see all these realities of Paradise suddenly burst into flower, in the midst of her wretchedness! She looked as if stunned at the person who was speaking, and could only sob two or three times: "Oh, oh, oh!" Her legs gave way, she fell on her knees before M. Madeleine, and before he could prevent it, he felt her seize his hand and press her lips to it.

Then she fainted.

(To be continued.)

Are Strikes and Trade Unions Injurious to the Laboring Classes?

REPLY TO ARTICLES OF W. G. H. SMART, RECENTLY PUBLISHED IN "THE LABOR REVIEW."

Like the contributors of the leading literary reviews, who every few months demolish (to their own satisfaction) the arguments in favor of Socialism, and after each attack find it necesshry to repeat the process, Comrade Smart again takes up the cudgel to smash the Trade Union movement. We know that his intension is a laudable one, namely, to convince the workingmen that the wage-system itself must be destroyed before any material improvement of our condition can be hoped for. But unfortunately our friend cannot realize that. even when every Trade Unionist recognizes the evils of Capitalism and the benefits of Socialism, the battle still remains to be fought. The wage system and its paralyzing influences, its oppressive conditions, must still be overcome. And while wage-slavery exists, the slaves must have organization to equalize the burdens occasioned by fluctuations of market prices, even if material improvement of the life-standard were impossible. That such organization can and does succeed in reducing the working time and increasing the wages, Comrade Smart admits. (He will, however, meet with a sharp criticism from his friend Haller, for this admission.) To tell the truth, our friend's admission has rendered the task of confuting his closing argument, one of little difficulty. These admissions may be enumerated as follows:

1. Through strikes and trades unions have been gained a gradual rise in wages and reduction of the hours of labor—*a gain not produced by other causes*, and the general effect has been to advance wages of all kinds of labor everywhere.

2. A still greater gain has arisen from the increased power afforded to the laboring classes through their organization alone.

From the above concessions, the conclusion must naturally follow that so long as the wage system exists, there will be direct benefits accruing to each individual through trade union organizations.

These direct, positive, and certain benefits can be gained by *no other* form of organization while the workmen remain wage workers. Only those who form cooperative associations can possibly escape the need of their Trade Unions and then by an improved form of union. But small co-operative associations cannot long exist in competition with great capitalistic enterprises in the same trade, as Lassalle has ably demonstrated. Even if the State refuses to recog-

hold on to your trades unions!" And there he weakens. He knows of no alternative. He offers none. He cannot offer any. The ballot is no alternative for the strike. The political party is no substitute for the trade union. The rate of wages cannot be regulated by law, nor the hours of labor shortened by law alone, while all industry is in the hands of capitalists, and at last Comrade Smart despairingly says: "if the unions were conducted in a different spirit, for a different purpose; if all would resolve to strike on a certain day, once and forever, then I should have faith in trades unions." But he has no such expectation. He sees in trades unions no tendency in that direction. Alas, none are so blind as those who will not see. After admitting that unions bring sure and positive benefits, thus being organizations which must draw to them wages workers of every political faith for their class interests, no matter whether they have hitherto voted the Republican, Democratic or Socialist tickets—after admitting (by offering no substitute) that nothing can take the place of the trade union in the contest with employers, he tries to save his case by a weak assertion. Let us see whether the trade unions have no tendency toward final emancipation.

(Concluded next month.)

THERE must be for human affairs an order which is the best. This order is by no means always the existing one; else why should we all

A Great Danger.

The stomach is the point to which all eyes are directed, when a person is "on a strike." Now, if Dr. Tanner proves by experience that a person can go without eating for forty days, the rule of the bosses will be in great danger; for what employer can hold out against men who can go without eating for six weeks at a "stretch?" Dr. Tanner, without knowing it, is circumventing the most fatal fact that tells against labor. Says the *Irish World*: "Once demonstrate that eating is a mere conventional custom which can easily be dispensed with at pleasure, and no soulless corporation will ever again attempt to hold out against a strike. The wolf will slink away from the laborer's door, never to return. Let men once successfully set the example of not eating, and Profits will speedily follow their example. They will no longer eat out the vitals of Labor, for it is the artificial Supply and Demand of thieves which creates them and their appetites.

"The experiment of Dr. Tanner is a terrible ordeal for profit-mongers, from the undertakers up. As George Francis Train, in his last dispatch to him, says: "Butchers, bakers, grocers as well as doctors, are 'cornered' in your success!"

"But the worst cornered man will be the Political Economist. He will be glad to vomit up the old sophisms of Supply and Demand, since it will refuse henceforth to fight the battles of his patron and ally, the Capitalist. Take the necessities of the stomach out of the fight, and strikes will batter down the world if employers insist on turning a deaf ear to equity and justice. All honor to Dr. Tanner! May his forty days of fasting lengthen into forty years, and open to the vision of Labor the promised land of peace and plenty."

The Beauties of English Orthography.

The following jingle may be of interest to our German friends. It brings into close proximity words having the same sound but with different meanings.

A pretty deer is dear to me,
A hare with downy hair;
A hart I love with all my heart,
But barely bear a bear.

'Tis plain that no one takes a plane
To shave a pair of pears,
Although a rake may take a rake
To tear away the tares.

A scribe in writing right may write
To write and still be wrong;
For write and rite are neither right,
And don't to right belong.

Robertson is not Robert's son
Nor did he rob Burt's son;
Yet Robert's son is Robin's son,
And everybody's sun.

Beer often brings a bier to man,
Coughing a coffin brings;
Ann too much ale will make us all,
As well as other things.

The person lies who says he lies
When he is not reclining;
And when consumptive folks decline,
They all decline declining.

Quails do not quail before a storm,
A bough will bow before it;
We cannot rein the rain at all,
No earthly power reigns o'er it.

The dyer dyes awhile, then dies—
To dye he's always trying;
Until upon his dying bed
He thinks no more of dyeing

A son of Mars mars many a son,
All Days must have their day;
And every knight should pray each night
To him who weighs his ways.

'Tis meet that man should mete out meat,
To feed one's fortune's son;
The fair should fare on love alone,
Else one cannot be won.

Alas, a lass is sometimes false,
Of faults a maid is made;
Her waist is but a barren waste—
Though stayed she is not staid.

The spring shoots forth each spring and
Shoot forward one and all;   [shoots
Though summer kills the flowers,it leaves
The leaves to fall in fall.

Itwould a story here commence,
But you might think it stale;
So we'll suppose that we have reached
The tail end of our tale.

Comrade Fowler, of Providence, R. I., writes that the Greenback Socialists intend to make things lively there this fall.

The Dollar.

Dollar is the name of a coin, and the unit in the monetary system of the United States. The origin of the name deserves notice. *Dollar* is a variety of the Ger. *thaler*, Low Ger. *dahler*, Dan. *daler*; and the word came to signify a coin thus: about the end of the 15th century, the Counts of Schlick coined the silver extracted from their silver mines at Joachims-thal (Joachim's valley) into ounce pieces, which received the name of Joachim-thaler—the Ger. adjective from the name of the place (Joachim's-dalers, as it were). These coins gained such a reputation that they became a sort of pattern, and others of the same kind, though made in other places, took the name, only dropping the first part of the word, for shortness. The American dollar is taken from the old Spanish dollar or piastre, and is only slightly less. It was formerly only of silver; but in 1873 the gold dollar was made the unit of value in the United States. In 1878, however, silver was 'remonitized,' and so now shares with gold the rank of standard money. Since 1837, the silver dollar is required to contain 412 1-2 troy grains, 26.4246 Fr. grammes, the fineness of which is fixed at 9-10, i. e., 1-10 of it is alloy. In the standard silver of Great Britain 1-12 is alloy. The United States dollar is generally estimated in exchange at 4s. 2d. sterling. Besides dollars there are coined in silver, *half-dollars*, *quarter-dollars*, *dimes* (1-10 dol.), *half-dimes* (1-20 dol.), and three-cent pieces. With regard to these, it was enacted in 1853 that the weight of the half-dollar should be 192 grains, and that of the others in proportional to this; and that such silver coins shall be legal tender for all sums not exceeding five dollars. Accounts are kept in dollars and cents, or hundredths of a dollar which are written thus: $13.73—

thirteen dollars and seventy-three cents. The standard gold of the United Stated is of the same fineness as the silver—namely 9-10; and of this are coined double eagles, eagles, half-eagles, and quarter-eagles, of 20, 10, 5, and 2 1-2 dollars, besides three-dollar and one dollar pieces. The dollar or thaler in Germany had various values. That of Prussia, which was most current was equivalant to 3s. sterling.—*Chamber's Encyclopœdia.*

Notes by the Way.

GENERAL WEAVER says he is sure the Greenback Labor Party "will carry Alabama, Arkansas, Mississippi, Texas and some of the Northern States." If they carry any three States, it will throw the election into the House of Representatives, in which case De la Matyr, the Greenback congressman, will have the deciding vote.

SOME of the young women employed in the caustic soda department of salt works at Southwark, Pa., chalked on a tank: "Our choice for President, Gen. Winfield S. Hancock." The Superintendent discharged the whole lot, as he was unable to find out the particular one guilty of the crime of having anti-Republican sympathies.

THE rope makers and spinners numbering nearly 500 who struck at Brooklyn, N. Y., ropeworks for higher wages, still continue on strike in spite of the warnings of their late employers, that if they do not speedily return to work, they cannot return at all. The strikers say they cannot subsist on the present low rate of wages, and will seek work in other factories and at different kinds of business before they will resume work at the old rates.

GEORGE RIPLEY, a charter member of the Brooks Farm Community, and literary editor of the New York

Tribune, is dead. He was a Socialist of most advanced views. The *N. Y. Sun* in eulogizing his life and recording his death, speaking of his belief in Democratic principles says: "The faith of democracy, the faith of humanity, the faith that mankind are steadily growing towards a society not of antagonism but of concord, not of artificial distinctions but of spiritual development, towards a society commanding the forces of external nature and converting the earth into an abode of peace and beauty, excelling the mythical Eden of old: this we say still lives among men. The mortal remains of Ripley were to-day committed to the earth; but the faith survives immortal and consoling."

IN Great Britain the labor market is dull, both the iron and coal trade showing considerable depression. At the shipbuilding and northern ports business may be called brisk, but in the textile trades everything is quiet or dull, especially in the lace and hosiery branches. At Macclesfield the silk trade is poor.

THE Chicago printers have been assessed $2 on those holding weekly sits. and 10 per cent. on those working by the piece to pay for the International jamboree. The book offices are on strike, and the bosses state they will sacrifice $10,000 to beat the union.

THE furniture workers of New York city are on strike against an increase in the hours of labor. They are now on their eighth week, and have just resolved by secret ballot to persist to the last in their determination to work only nine hours a day.

THE Albany, N. Y., cigarmakers have obtained an advance.

JOHN SWINTON has gone on a visit to France.

Subscribe for the LABOR REVIEW.

SOCIALISTIC LABOR PARTY.

NATIONAL EXECUTIVE COMMITTEE.

P. C. Christiansen........128 Antoine st.
Charles Erb............579 Dequinde st.
Judson Grenell..........116 Howard st.
Gustav Herzig...........39 Napoleon st.
Philip Van Patten........P. O. Box 597
E. W. Simpson, Rec.Sec'y..90 Wilkins st.
Wm. Kuess............556 Clinton ave.

The New Board of Supervision.

The National Board of Supervision is composed of the following seven members elected by the section of Brooklyn, N. Y.: H. Gottschalk, F. Fuchs, F. Paul, Chr. Patberg, Joseph Holler, — Hildebrand and Wm. Wagner. The last named has been elected secretary. His address is Wm. Wagner, 42 Stagg st., Brooklyn.

General Party News.

DROPPINGS FROM HEADQUARTERS.

The Section of New Haven sent delegates to the Greenback Convention of Connecticut, under instructions similar to those governing our delgates to the National Convention. A sound Labor Platform was the result.

In Massachusetts the Sections are waiting to learn the result of the Party vote on the question of supporting the Greenback Presidental nominee this fall. Until something definite is known, agitation is postponed.

The Boston Section is still weak, owing to the pride and vanity of the "great minds" who are too anxious for personal distinction to submit themselves to the Section regulations. Come, friends, sink your differences and stand by the Party.

The Brooklyn Section has elected the seven members who compose the National Board of Supervision. Their names are published elsewhere. Osborn Ward is ready to take the field as an agitator and makes the following very liberal offer: He will visit any Section, neighboring Section, or the sections on a continuous line from New York to Chicago and from Cincinnati to Baltimore, on condition that those Sections shall order of him all necessary lecture tickets, posters, etc., and he will print the articles at regular prices. With the proceeds of this work and the sale of his books, he will pay his own traveling expenses. As soon as the Party vote is announced he will strike out. His address is 610 Bergen St., Brooklyn. Give him a call!

New York Socialists are greatly excited over the questions now being voted upon. A strong element is making a bitter fight against coalition or joint action of any kind, in common with the Greenback Labor Party. Unfortunately the discussion has reached the verge of an actual warfare, in which the motives of the contesting parties are being impugned in a style calculated to cause a permanent breach. Dr. Douai, editor of our daily German paper, and Comrade Bunata, editor of the Bohemian Party organ, have both published solemn warnings, appealing for the restoration of a proper spirit of fraternity, and asking that the questions be discussed on their own merits, without personalties. The vote will probably be in the negative.

Philadelphia has voted to support the Greenback Presidental Candidates. Comrade Wildmann is active in the Trades Assembly and convince

comrades should all read it. The National Executive Committee has a quantity on hand, to be sold at retail only.

Buffalo Socialists are preparing for an active campaign. They anxiously desire to vote against the capitalistic power, and had even prepared to form local connection with the Greenback Labor Party, but refrained on request of the National Executive Committee, as the Party vote has not yet been announced. Comrade Pollner, of Cleveland, delivered an able address at the picnic held July 6th. Our weekly paper is doing well under the managment of Comrade Erhardt.

Pottsville, Pa., Greenbackers are strongly tinged with Socialism. One of their prominent speakers asks for tracts, pamphlets, etc., and says that as the Greenback Party is now compelled to defend Socialism the men must be instructed. (Who says the Socialists gain nothing by joint action?)

In Cincinnati there will soon be another Section. Comrade Murphy is stirring up the old members who withdrew when the "purifiers" commenced the work of "reform." A visit from Comrade McGuire is in anticipation, excellent results being looked for. John Ehmann is doing editorial work for the *Exponent*, the organ of the Cincinnati Trades Assembly, and the ablest Trade Union newspaper in the West. Comrade Goehler is over all his troubles and has assumed a foreman's position in the Safe Factory.

from Socialists. Let workingmen run their own affairs! An excursion will be given on the 25th inst. Sugar Island being engaged for the festivities. The Trades Assembly has resolved to petition the City Council for free bathing institutions. The Iron Moulders are being flattered and bribed by Democratic polticians, their votes being the prizes coveted. This work is infamous, and will soon be exposed.

The Tract Association has published and sold 210,000 tracts since commencement of the enterprise one year ago. No better means of agitation can be devised! A lot of new tracts will appear in a short time.

Indianapolis members believe that the Greenback candidates should be supported this Fall on account of the oportunities offered us for agitation. Comrade McGuire will soon visit this place on an agitation tour. J. F. Brown has delivered a very able address on Socialism—andComrade Lizius published it in the *Irish World*. Let the example be followed whenever possible, for the *Irish World* will publish all articles worthy of consideration upon Socialistic topics.

The Milwaukee section has ordered a lot of tracts and will now prosecute a lively warfare on Capitalism. Since our daily paper, the *Journal* was enlarged, its editor, Comrade Biron, reports increased prosperity.

St. Louis remains a lively center of labor agitation. The Trades Unions are active and aggressive. Our Section has had considerable trouble on account of the daily paper *Volkes Stimme*, which had been so poorly managed that it was compelled to suspend. Dr. Walster has again resumed the editorial chair, however, and issues a weekly which it is to be hoped will succeed better than the last. Comrade McGuire visited the Greenback State Convention of Missouri, the other day and

did glorious work for our cause. The Platform starts out with a good declaration on the Land Question, and contains many other radical expressions and demands. Comrade McGuire was offered invitations to address Greenback meetings in over twenty different towns throughout the State, but declined all except two. His next trip will be to Evanville, Indianapolis, Louisville and possibly Cincinnati under the National Executive Committee.

NEW ORLEANS is fast becoming a second San Francisco as a labor stronghold. They have no "sand lot" but places just as good, and instead of one Kearney they have 20 —not so demonstrative, perhaps, but just as earnest and active. Comrade Geissler has succeeded in establishing such firm connections between the section and the trades unions that they send representatives to a joint assembly and publish an able English weekly in common. The paper is called the *Workingmen's Union Advocate*, and is as much a Socialistic organ as we could desire.

SAN FRANCISCO workingmen now suffer from a cunning attack of the Democratic demagogues, who have succeeded in gaining the services of some expelled would-be leaders of the W. P. C. These rascals attempted to mob Kearney on the Sand Lot and have gone so far as to call themselves the W. P. C. itself, and as such to endorse the Democratic ticket. They have, however, only Democratic "blowers" and "strikers" for supporters—men who now "belong" to the Workingmen's Party for the first time in their lives. Our section has rallied to assist in crushing these vipers, and has established friendly relations with the liberal element of the Workingmen's Party of California. It is only a question of time when Kearney and the true labor men of the Pacific Coast will be shoulder to shoulder with us. The future is ours !

The Chicago Muddle.

Chicago, the scene of our greatest triumphs, is just now the field of some of the most sorrowful battles in which our members have ever sullied their weapons. One daily German paper, which previous to and during the Greenback Convention was enthusiastic for coalition and prophesied useful opportunities for spreading our principles, suddenly changed front when there was a prospect of harmony in the party. Harmony is not what is wanted, therefore, the paper has commenced so furious an attack upon the Greenback Party, and denounces so bitterly the movement for joint action with our Party that the entire Section is split up. The proposed alliance is now called "amalgamation." The delegates of our Party who reported favorably and who advocated the alliance, are called "compromisers," "conspirators," and "Greenback agents." Among these conspirators are the men who built up the Party and struggled for years before the editor of the "*Arbeter Zeitung*" ever saw this country—such men as P. J. McGuire, Dr. A. Douai, T. J. Morgan, Geo. Winter, George Schilling, John McAuliffe, and many others. For the manner in which the paper is alleged to have missrepresented the Convention and its results, and of committing other misdeeds, the editor, Paul Grottkau, and Peter Peterson, editor of the Scandinavian weekly, were both expelled from the Chicago Section conditional upon the ratification of this action by the next section meeting. The manner of the expulsion was so unwise, having been abrupt and without any process of trial, that the editors found sympathizers among the German members; so at the next meeting (alleged to have been a Section meeting) the vote of expulsion was rescinded, and Peter Peterson and others of the opposition were elected as Section officers. The English speaking Branch and the former Section officers protested against these actions, claiming that the meeting was illegally called. The dispute has been submitted to the National Board of Supervsion for settlement. The entire affair is deplorable, and would never have happened had our members reflected coolly, and promptly squelched the war of personalities in the beginnig. Our Party press and especially the Chicago papers has enjoyed so much "freedom," that some of the editors have attacked reputations, thrown mud, and misrepresented facts, whenever they felt disposed. The Constitution of our Party seem a dead letter, so far as they are concerned. If this last occurrence does not result in a thorough reform in the editorial managment, we fear that Democratic rule within our Party may become "Demagogic" rule, and instead of free discussion, we may have free denunciation. These criticisms are so necessary at this time that silence would be criminal. Discussion upon Party matters, require no personal denunciation nor any impugnment of each other's motives. If the Party desires to support the Greenback Presidential ticket, it will not have been caused by any "conspiring" other than the "conspiracy" of the whole Party, when by a nearly unanimous vote, our Sections resolved to send delegates to the Chicago Convention. If the Party votes down the proposed alliance, such action will not mean that the Republican Party has purchased our German leaders, but merely that we are not yet prepared for coalition. Until our Sections are so well organized and disciplined that they can trust their members in any alliance, and can discuss the advisability of such steps without mutual recrimination, we are unprepared and unfit to undertake any such coalitions. There.

fore it may be best that for the present, at least, our Party should remain strictly independent, as was decided by our last Convention at Alleghany.

Financial Report of the National Executive Committee for the Month of June, 1880.

RECEIPTS.

Rockville, Conn., Section, dues.... $3 30
Paterson, N. J.,   do 10 09
St. Joseph, Mo.,   do 1 60
Evansville, Ind·,   do 10 00
Boston, Mass.,   do 2 35
Baltimore, Md.,   do 6 85
New York city, N.Y., do 75 00
Alleghany, Pa.,   do 3 75
G. Lizius, Indianapolis, convention
  reports........................ 1 00
Buffalo, N. Y., Section, dues..... 1 00
New Orleans, La., Section, dues... 7 15
Streator, Ill., John Keay......... 1 00
Streator, Ill.,John Keay,pamphlets. 1 00
Philadelphia, Pa., Section, dues... 6 85
Secretary Van Patten, pamphlets... 50
Jersey City, N. Y., Section—
  German Branch................. 5 20
  English-speaking Branch....... 2 15
Fewark, N. J., Section, dues...... 8 70
John G. Drew Trenton, N. J., pamphlets...................... 1 00

Total.....................$148 40

EXPENDITURES.

Current expenses, postage, printing, etc........................ 21 23
Co-operating Printers............. 2 25
Secretary's Chicago trip (traveling expenses)...................... 11 00
W. C. Pollner, agitation trip...... 10 00
Salary of Secretary, five weeks 60 00

Total.......................$104 48

SOCIALISTIC PAMPHLETS.—Better Times, by Dr. A. Douai, 5 cts; Lasalle's Open Letter, (translation), 10 cts; Coming Revolution, by L. B. Groenlund, 15 cts; Labor Catechism, by Osborn Ward, 25 cts; Capital, (extracts,) by Karl Marx, 20 cts; Does Socialism tend to Abolish Private Property? by John Ehmann, 5 cents; Why the State should Create a Bureau of Labor Statistics, by P. J. McGuire, 5 cts.
Address   PHILIP VAN PATTEN,
      P. O. Box 597, Detroit, Mich.

NOTICE.—The official report of the last National Convention of our party are published in pamphlet form, together with the new platform and constitution. Price, 10c. Address all orders to Philip Van Pattern, Party Secretary, P. O. Box 597 Detroit, Mich.

210,000.

The above is the number of tracts the Socialistic Tract Association have sold the past thirteen months. The supply is exhausted for the present but a lot of new tracts will be printed, as well as some of the old, as soon as a demand springs up that will justify it.

THE Statistician of the Agricultural Department, Col. Worthington, has finished his annual report on farm labor wages, in which he states that in the Pacific and mining States and Territories the range of monthly wages for farm laborers, without board, is between $30.75 and $22.50. Minnesota pays her farm laborers better wages than any other state: $16.33, with board. Vermont pays only $12.62. In the Southern states the average is $9.60. He gives the average cost of subsistance per month to the laborer at $7.17 for 1880 against 7.14 for 1879. "Heretofore in the decline of wages, the cost of subsistence declined in quite the same ratio, but for this year the proportion is largely in favor of the laborer, as the cost of subsistence remains nearly at the lowest rate, while the wages has materially advanced."

Let it be established as a fact in our labor system that the employes of the land will not, under any circumstances, resist to the extent of striking, any policy their employers may see fit to inaugurate, and how long would it be before the united labors of father, mother and children would not place the common necesaries of life upon the table of the toiler.—*Denver Argus.*